Maribeth Adams trembled on the bed, clutching the comforter around her naked body. "Hey, Sebastian," she called, lowering the blanket to her waist and letting her luscious breasts bob free.

The Mexican's leering gaze lingered longer than it should have over her seminude body. His grip unconsciously lightened on Cord's body. Cord's hand swept the floor for a weapon. His fingers grasped something smooth and hard, the champagne bottle Maribeth had sitting on the card table last evening. I'm glad that it's still full, he thought.

Cord swung the champagne in a smooth arc, shattering the glass across the giant's temple. The exploding bottle sounded like a rifle shot as the sparkling wine sprayed across the room. The liquid soaked Corazón's blouse, making the silky fabric cling to her shapely breasts. Sebastian toppled to the floor. He rose slowly, holding his bleeding head and staggering about the room. Cord pushed the reeling giant toward the open window.

"Please no, señor," Corazón begged . . .

Other books in the DIAMONDBACK series from Pinnacle

DIAMONDBACK

#4

DEAD MAN'S HAND
by PIKE BISHOP

PINNACLE BOOKS ⊚ NEW YORK

This is a work of fiction. All the characters and events portrayed in
this book are fictional, and any resemblance to real people or
incidents is purely coincidental.

DIAMONDBACK #4: DEAD MAN'S HAND

Copyright © 1984 by Raymond Obstfeld

An original Pinnacle Books edition, published for the first time
anywhere.

First printing/June 1984

ISBN: 0-523-42200-8

Can. ISBN: 0-523-43190-2

Cover art by Aleta Jenks

Printed in the United States of America

PINNACLE BOOKS, INC.
1430 Broadway
New York, New York 10018

9 8 7 6 5 4 3 2 1

An acknowledgment is made to the contributions of Gene Garofalo for his assistance on this book.

1.

"You can still chicken out." The foreman smirked.

"Cluck, cluck," someone behind him said. The other hands laughed.

Cord Diamondback tugged the cracked leather chaps over his legs. The stiff batwings creaked in protest as he heaved them past his thighs. Not a new outfit, Cord thought. Hand-me-downs for the new hand.

"It don't mean nothing to me if you're aching to get yourself killed," the foreman, Rancel Krups, continued. "But I won't have you upsetting the horses. They're worth money." Krups's broad grin faded for a moment. "Seriously, you got any idea of what you're doing?"

Cord smiled tightly, trying to look confident. "What I'm doing is earning money. The poster I saw advertised five dollars for every mustang that's broken."

Krups's face screwed in doubt. "You just ain't got the look of a bronc peeler. If you claimed you was a gambler or gunfighter, I'd buy that story in a minute. But you ain't got the gait of a man who's spent most of his life rolling around the backs of wild horses."

"What does it take to convince you? Bowed legs? A fistful of broken fingers?"

"Wouldn't hurt. Most of the great bronc riders wear them badges."

Cord's cash had run dry. He needed money and there wasn't a judging job in sight. He couldn't even rustle up a prizefight because he had nothing to put up as a stake.

Six months earlier, Cord's saddlebags had bulged with greenbacks after a lucrative judging job and two prizefight victories in a row. He treated himself to a winter in New Orleans, as far east as he dared go without risking meeting old friends. The Creole aristocrat he met there, Madelina, had introduced him to New Orleans society. Silk and champagne and other sensuous pleasures were a normal part of her life. Cord still carried pleasant memories of gay parties in lush surroundings followed by sultry nights alone with Madelina. She treated him as a pet, unwilling to let him spend any of his money.

Cord's bankroll was still intact at the time of the all-or-nothing prizefight with Armondo, a Cajun only half Cord's size. Cord bet every penny he could beat the wiry bayou rat. A win seemed certain, the Cajun was such a small man. But Armondo had tricks that Cord hadn't seen before: like kicking a man in the face from a standing position. Cord's jaw still ached when he thought about the match.

Madelina remained true. "Stay here, *cheri*," she begged. "I have money enough for us both."

"Thank you," Cord said, kissing her just above

the point where her olive-colored breasts jutted from her chest. "I've never had a more tempting offer." But one season was all Cord Diamondback dared spend in any town. Longer and he risked some curious busybody digging into his past.

The promise of a well-paying judging job sent Cord riding to New Mexico. He arrived to find the quarreling parties had killed one another, settling their dispute with more finality than any judgment from Diamondback. Now, Cord needed money to replace his Smith & Wesson Schofield .44. A cowtown bully felt challenged by Cord's quiet assurance and ragged him into a fight. A crease across the side of his skull from the barrel of Cord's revolver had taught the bully some manners, but the gun hadn't worked right since.

Cord knew that taming wild broncs was profitable, but it could also be painful. A jarring ride from a rough mustang could scramble a man's insides, dislocate his neck and spine, turn his body into a mass of bruises. Cord had seen some bronc riders bleeding from the mouth and ears an hour after a successful ride. Riders had dismounted from apparently tamed broncs and fainted. Bronc riding was dangerous all right, but that's why it offered more opportunity than signing on as a ranch hand for twenty-five dollars a month.

"Let's forget about the sparring," Cord told Krups. "Are you paying the rates advertised?"

"I pay the five dollars per horse *after* they're gentled." Krups shifted a chaw of tobacco from place to place inside his mouth as if the wad kept wearing out its welcome. "That could come to less than a buck per broken rib if you don't know your business. What experience you got? A bad ride by a rank amateur makes a bronc tougher to break."

"Did you ever see Cody's Wild West show?"

Krups's jaw dropped. "You was with the Congress of Rough Riders?"

"I've been inside the tent a few times." That much was true. Cord had been a spectator at several of Cody's shows.

Krups put his face close to Cord's and gave him a whiff of the sour breath that caused the ranch hands to call him "Rancid" Krups. "Anybody can say he rode in Cody's parade. I ain't letting you spoil a good pony until I see what you can do on a bad one."

Cord smiled to himself, seeing where the foreman was headed. "A bad one, huh? I have a hunch that this is my lucky day because you have a particular animal in mind."

Krups's face went bland, the smirk drifting out of it like smoke away from a campfire. "Just so happens there's a tryout horse we use when anyone comes riding in here claiming to be a bronc peeler. A real professional such as yourself shouldn't have any trouble keeping his butt plastered atop Heelkicker. He's such a gentle creature."

"Heelkicker? Something tells me his name is meant to be descriptive."

"We'll see what you want to call him after the ride. Providing you still got teeth to talk through."

I've taken on too much, Cord thought. Krups was obviously setting him up for a ride on the local fire-eating stallion. Cord saw that the foreman hoped he would fail and was stacking the deck by putting him on board some notorious boneshaker.

Cord had some experience riding wild mounts. He had lived for a season with those master horsemen, the Shoshone Indians, who had given him the name Diamondback. For the brief time he had adopted their way of life; he'd gone with them on their hunts and learned some of their skills, but he never mastered the way the Shoshones managed to make horse and rider meld into one animal. That was a skill that couldn't be taught; it was something that had to be lived for generations.

"I ain't expecting you to stay on Heelkicker for long," Krups said indulgently. "No one has. I'm just anxious to see how professional and elegant you look when you come flying off."

"I see you're more interested in form than substance."

"Huh?"

"Forget it," Cord said. A discussion on style versus accomplishment might be appropriate for the Harvard yard, but not here.

Krups frowned and spit a wad of tobacco that splattered on the ground and formed a small brown puddle next to Cord's boots. "Save them odd remarks for Heelkicker. Maybe he'll give you a horse laugh."

A one-story bunkhouse constructed of roughly cut pine logs chinked with clay and covered by a sod roof stood twenty yards from the corral. Two men lounged in the open door of the bunkhouse oiling their Winchesters. Another man washed potatoes and carrots in a wooden barrel near the chuckhouse which sat behind the bunkhouse another ten feet from the corral. Four cowboys inside the corral checked out their gear in preparation for the day's work.

Krups cupped his weather-beaten hands and called to the men. "Hey, boys, we got entertainment today. Here's a hot rider from God knows where who's going to get up on Heelkicker's back just so he can teach us a little something about bronc riding."

The cowboys dropped what they were doing, exchanged broad grins, and climbed to the top rung of the corral fence. A few, working without hats, used their hands to shade their eyes from the afternoon sun as they turned toward the inner corral that penned the ranch's working horses.

One of the men working the corral walked up to Cord. His skin, burned and cured from long hours in the New Mexico sun, had the color and texture of saddle leather. The man stood no taller than five and a half feet, including the three-inch heels on his boots. Cord noticed the boots were cut high to protect the man's calves from chafing against the stirrup strap. The bootheels sloped inward so they wouldn't catch on the saddle stirrups if he fell while riding. Underneath his chaps, which were in better shape than Cord's loaners, he wore cheap sackcloth trousers fastened with a twine belt. A real working cowboy, Cord thought.

"I'm Marty," the small man said, flashing a friendly smile and throwing his arm out toward Cord. "If you're going for a spin on Heelkicker, be careful after you're throwed. That animal will stomp any man laying on the ground just like he would stomp on a rattler. If you ain't out of the corral fast enough, he'll kick you to pieces." Marty inspected Cord with a lazy grin. "Why are you doing this anyway?"

"I love animals."

Marty nodded. "Hard up for cash, hey? That's the usual reason. I think it's kinda dumb. The last man who got up on that stallion had his spine cracked. He still ain't walking and I can't see how the injury improved his financial condition."

"I appreciate the warning."

"Marty," Krups called impatiently. "We're keeping this hotshot waiting and we're all anxious for the lesson he's going to give us. Get Heelkicker out here."

The tiny man waved at Krups, flicked the tiniest of winks at Cord, and climbed aboard a gray gelding who had been tied to the corral fence. He signaled another cowboy to open the gate and urged the gelding inside, lifting his lasso from the saddle and trailing it along the ground as the gelding trotted in, kicking up tiny puffs of dust.

"I'm surprised you're keeping a stallion with the other horses," Cord told one of the nearby cowboys.

"Ain't no mares in there," the cowboy answered, keeping a close eye on Marty. "No other stallions either. The rest is all geldings so the herd don't get nervous."

As Marty guided his gelding toward the horses, Cord scanned the herd, anxious for the first look at his ride. The horses scattered and bolted until a magnificent stallion, a dark smoky gray, the same shade as a mesquite campfire, broke free from the crowd. Cord estimated the stallion stood nearly sixteen hands high. He galloped away from the geldings, moving as fluidly as a rolling sea, a machine with his body on springlike joints.

The stallion skidded and wheeled within the confines of the small corral, showing the strength in his sleek muscles as he tried to keep distance between him and the rider tracking him down. His black liquid eyes were uncomprehending but defiant as he sought out the far reaches of the corral.

Marty's well-trained gelding allowed the cowboy to use both hands on the lasso as he guided the horse with his knees. Christ, I'm watching *real* professionals, Cord thought with admiration. The thought made him feel suddenly a little ashamed, even foolish.

Marty skillfully cut down the corral on Heelkicker until the animal was cornered. The stallion stood his ground now, rearing his head high and flaring his nostrils.

"You got him now, cowboy," one of the hands sitting on the fence hollered toward the corral. His voice sounded deep and rough, as if it had been sifted through a throatful of gravel before leaving his mouth.

Krups turned toward Cord with a look of gleeful anticipation. "We're about ready to accommodate you," he said. He scanned Cord's lean body. "I hope you know how to cushion a fall. Your frame don't look too well padded to me."

"I bounce well," Cord said. "Providing I land on my head."

Cord wondered if he had landed on his head when he got involved in this situation. Maybe he should walk away. Why should he provide a free exhibition for the amusement of a few cowboys? He looked at the men sitting on the corral fence and nudging one another. He didn't feel the need to prove anything to these guys. If he was lucky he'd come out of the afternoon with a mass of bumps and bruises and maybe five bucks. If he was unlucky, who knows? Still he needed money, a new pistol was vital to his survival, and he had to ride the local legend to get it. One look at the rearing, snorting animal gave Cord a dry taste in his mouth, as if he'd chewed on a sawdust steak.

Marty made small clicking noises as he closed on the cornered stallion. His lasso still trailed behind him on the ground. Heelkicker snorted a warning when the cowboy rode too close. The gelding stopped and stood quiet as Marty rose in his stirrups and flipped a small loop over the stallion's head. The rope slipped down easily until it rested where Heelkicker's neck met his shoulders. Once the lasso brushed against the horse's smoke-gray hide, he bolted as if he'd been stung by a bee. Marty calmly held the rope until the slack of the coils played out, then turned the lasso twice around his saddle horn. The gelding dug in his heels and skidded across the gravel of the corral, stopping Heelkicker short.

The wild horse snorted and reared high again, giving Cord an unwelcome look at sharp hooves capable of slicing through an arm or leg. Marty urged his gelding to retreat, keeping the lariat taut as the stallion tried to break free.

Marty backed the gelding toward a snubbing post dug into the ground near one end of the corral. He unwound the rope from the saddle horn and tied it to the post, leaving the stallion tugging at his bonds as he trotted his gelding out the corral gate.

"Nice job, Marty," the gravelly-voiced cowboy approved, clapping his hand to his thigh. Cord noticed that most of the cowboys had turned and squinted toward him expectantly.

"Your turn now," Marty said as he dismounted and tied up his gelding. "Putting on the reins and saddle is a job for the bronc buster. I'm buying a seat on the corral fence."

"I'm sure it'll help me get to know the animal better," Cord said, moving toward the corral.

Cord approached Heelkicker slowly, watching in awe as the snubbing post rattled and bent from the force of the horse's effort to break free. "Neither of us wants to be here," he whispered as he neared the animal. "So let's make this as quick as possible. Painless would be nice too."

The stallion tugged at the rope binding him to the snubbing post, his smoke-gray flanks covered with foamy sweat. Cord stepped around toward the animal's head, hiding a hackamore bridle behind his back. As Heelkicker fought against the rope, Cord quickly slipped the bridle over the horse's head. The hackamore was a good training bridle because it had a loop that could be tightened around the stallion's nose, taking the place of a bit.

Heelkicker shook his head mightily in an effort to shake off the nuisance, once thumping Cord hard in the chest with his neck. Cord felt the horse's strength as he went sprawling, his rib cage rattling against his internal organs. The blow felt harder than any he'd taken in the prize ring.

Cord held on to the bridle, forcing the stallion's head down as he threw a saddle blanket over his back. "I'll take it easy on you if you take it easy on me," Cord whispered. Great, he thought. Now I'm negotiating with a horse.

Heelkicker looked at Cord quizzically, as if he were evaluating the offer. He kicked up his hind legs, sending the saddle blanket into the dust and gravel of the corral, and pawed at it with his front hooves until Cord pulled on the bridle and forced him away.

"Your bones will be taking the place of that blanket, Diamondback," Krups shouted. "Providing you ever figure out how to get the horse saddled."

Cord waved toward Krups and carefully retrieved the saddle blanket. He made soothing noises as he gently replaced the cloth on Heelkicker's back. The horse eyed him suspiciously as Cord picked up his forty-pound, single-rigged saddle and threw it over the stallion's back, making sure the saddle skirt landed flush on the blanket.

The final and most dangerous step remained: the one where cowboys learned that horses had teeth and liked to bite. Cord reached around the stallion's head for the cinch ring on the far end of the saddle. Heelkicker appeared unconcerned as Cord fastened a latigo to the cinch ring. He reached beneath the horse and strapped on the saddle. Heelkicker was ready to ride.

A few scattered cheers drifted from the corral fence. "Remember what I told you," Marty warned. "When he knocks you off, get out of the corral fast."

"What makes you think I'm going to get knocked off?" Cord called back. "He seems tame enough to me." His remark triggered a chorus of hoots from the cowboys.

"Pull yourself into the saddle and do your bragging up there," Krups said impatiently. "That horse is as ready as he's ever going to be."

Cord wanted the ride now, anxious to match his skill against the stallion's wild strength. The fact that he was barely more than a novice bronc rider somehow excited him. Maybe he didn't have anything to prove to the others, but suddenly he wanted to prove something to himself.

Heelkicker stood strangely quiet, bearing the bridle and saddle with calm. His liquid eyes looked at Cord as if appraising this new challenger. His long face appeared confident; he had the look of an undefeated champion.

As Cord prepared to mount, he noticed a lanky stranger with straight black hair, the color of coal dust, approach the corral. The man climbed to the top of the corral fence and squatted next to the other men.

I know that man, Cord thought. The newcomer smoked a thin cheroot which he clenched tightly between white teeth. He was no ranch hand because he wore good-quality woolen trousers and a red-and-white-striped shirt. Over the shirt he sported a satin vest embroidered with daisies. The outfit might have caused laughter except for the leather holster strapped under his left armpit, which housed Colt's version of Henry Deringer's pocket-sized pistol. The barrel was only two-and-a-half inches long, but it had a large .44 bore that could blast a breeze way through a man's body at short range.

"What's going on here?" the lanky man asked with an easy grin.

"You came just in time," the gravelly-voiced

cowboy replied. "A good show's going on. Some damn fool is about to ride Heelkicker."

The man's grin spread until it covered his dark face. "That man's no fool. He bets with thin cards sometimes, but he's no fool."

He knows me, Cord thought. The hell with it, I'll worry about him later.

Krups glared over at the stranger. "The show ain't going to last long. That phony bronc rider is going to land in the dust the second after he gets aboard."

The stranger flicked ash from his cheroot. "I'll bet you a hundred dollars he stays on top for at least a minute."

"You're crazy! That's more than my month's wages as foreman."

"A man must have the strength of his convictions." The stranger smiled.

The conversation triggered Cord's memory. The lanky man was Deuce Devlin, the gambler who'd bet on anything. What was he doing in this part of New Mexico? There wasn't a game of chance within a hundred miles. But then Devlin usually made up his own games, and chance had nothing to do with them.

"Let's get going," Krups roared at Cord.

Cord put one foot into the stirrup. Heelkicker came alive, curling back his mouth and showing his teeth. He turned his head and tried to stuff Cord's arm between his jaws.

Cord tapped the stallion on the nose. "Try that again and I'll have horsemeat for supper."

Cord and the stallion danced for position with Cord skipping around the corral, one foot in the stirrup, the other in the dirt. The cowboys roared with laughter as Cord hopped on one leg and tried to steady Heelkicker.

Krups turned to Devlin. "I'll bet you fifty dollars. But the minute don't start until he's on the horse's back."

"It's a wager," Devlin said. "I've a weakness for the underdog."

Krups checked the faces of the cowboys near the corral and winked at the dude's stupidity.

Cord reached up and twisted Heelkicker's ear. The horse neighed and pulled his head down to escape from the pain. The brief second allowed Cord to steady his foot in the stirrup and swing his body around. He was finally on top of the horse.

Devlin pulled a Bulova railroad watch and showed the time to Krups and a few of the cowboys. "Fifty-nine seconds left."

Cord hoped to get fully aboard with both his feet securely in the stirrups before Heelkicker began bucking, but his butt barely caressed leather when the stallion exploded, seeming to turn his fluid body into an angry, choppy sea. Cord headed skyward, his only contact with earth the bridle he clutched in his hand.

Devlin snuffed out his cheroot and cupped his hands to his mouth. "Hey, Diamondback, why don't you stop abusing that poor animal? I've got a judging job for you."

"Now you tell me," Cord called back as his body hurled skyward again.

2.

Cord held the bridle tightly, his knuckles whitening as Heelkicker twisted under him. His muscles stretched into tight strings that stood out in relief against his forearm as he struggled to hang on to the bridle. It seemed to have a life of its own, like a writhing snake. Gravity took over and Cord descended fast, crashing on his butt toward the front of the saddle, the solid saddle horn grazing his testicles. Small shivers of pain swept through his groin. The stallion bucked again, all four feet off the ground, his body in a skyborne inverted U. Cord sailed up and down with the horse as if he were bobbing in the ocean aboard a small craft. His spine jolted a half-dozen times with shock waves speeding from his seat all the way up his back and cracking the nape of his neck like multiple rabbit punches.

"Look at that animal go sunfishing," Marty said admiringly.

"He's a real high roller," the gravelly-voiced cowboy agreed. His face beamed with happiness as he watched the legend live up to its reputation.

"He can't last much longer," Krups predicted.

"You mean the man or the horse?" Devlin asked.

Krups threw a contemptuous look toward the gambler. "That amateur peeler is going to land in the dust any second now."

"I'll wager an additional fifty dollars he stays on board for at least another minute," Devlin said with a lazy smile. "The man I mean."

"How long has he been up now?" Krups asked, grabbing at Devlin's watch.

"Thirty seconds."

"You got a bet. He looks done to me."

The stallion bucked his rear legs high, showing his hooves to the cowboys on the corral fence. Cord slapped his quirt onto Heelkicker's neck in a fast steady rhythm, hoping to calm him down.

Cord's feet desperately sought the stirrups. His left boot found a precarious hold when the horse reared so high he threatened to tumble over backward, landing hundreds of pounds of horseflesh on top of Diamondback. Cord lashed the stallion between the ears with his quirt until the animal stopped bucking. Heelkicker turned his head and bit Cord's free right leg, his long square teeth mashing into Cord's calf like a miller grinding corn. Cord kicked his spurs hard into Heelkicker's flank until the animal pulled his mouth away.

The stallion dipped his neck and head, pushing his nose toward the ground and forcing Cord to bend his body forward, balancing in the saddle. The stallion's powerful neck muscles pulled on the bridle, causing the leather to cut into Cord's palm like a dull knife sawing through the skin. His hand felt like he was squeezing the spear end of a harpoon.

Heelkicker twisted his body in a series of short, tight turns that made Cord feel he'd been sucked into a whirlpool. His head rocked with dizziness as his equilibrium left him. Cord tried to compensate by tilting in the direction of the turns only to have the stallion rear skyward again. Cord felt his body lifted out of the saddle as if he'd been plucked clean by a giant hand. He grabbed the bridle in both hands. The leather handle snapped off clean with a snap that was heard in the bunkhouse. Cord's lifeline to the earth was broken.

Cord landed half on, half off the saddle with Heelkicker turning his head as if surprised to see the rider still there. He snorted at the nuisance. Cord reached down and clutched the stallion's neck with both hands.

"That's not a proper ride," Krups declared. "I win the bet."

"He's not in the dirt," Devlin reminded the foreman.

Marty agreed. "The man's still in the saddle. His boots ain't touched the ground."

"How much time is left?" Devlin asked, retrieving his watch from Krups's hands. "I make it another thirty seconds before your money changes owners."

"You're nuts! There's no way any man can last thirty seconds aboard Heelkicker without a bridle."

"Did you want to redouble the bet then?"

"Err, no, I ain't out to steal your money."

Cord heard the exchange. He couldn't believe

he'd been aboard the horse for less than a minute. It seemed like hours.

Heelkicker took off at a fast gallop toward the corral fence. I can hang on, Cord thought, as long as he gallops over straight ground. The stallion turned at the fence, careening around the inner edge of the corral and deliberately crashing his huge body into the fence posts. Cord gritted his teeth as his right leg and arm were battered into the wooden posts. Wood slivers and bark knifed into his leg, wedging deep into his flesh. Pain flooded the area as if his leg had been hit by a heavy-gauge scattergun.

"Get off now, cowboy," Marty shouted. "You ain't the first man that horse has rode into the fence. He's too damn mean to be rode."

Cord tightened his grip on the horse's neck, twisting the mane with his left hand in a desperate effort to force the stallion back to the center of the corral. His face was plastered against the stallion's neck and the pungent animal smell, a crazy mixture of hay and manure, swept into his nostrils. Cord's cheek grew damp as his sweat mixed with the stallion's. Did the salty taste come from his body or Heelkicker's?

The stallion tried rearing high again, but Cord's weight prevented the animal from skying. He stomped out a short series of kicks with his rear legs, bucking and twisting as Cord held on desperately. The stallion tried to run for the fence again, but this time Cord pulled hard on his ear, forcing him back toward the center.

"Calm down," Cord whispered in Heelkicker's

ear. "In another few seconds this ride will be over for both of us."

"He ain't the most elegant bronc peeler I ever seen," Marty conceded. "But that cowboy is getting the job done."

"He's cheating," Krups exclaimed angrily. "I think Diamondback and this gambler are in this together to swindle me out of my money."

"Did you want the other side then?" Devlin asked. "Put up another twenty-five dollars and I'll let you switch your bet. You can have the cheating Diamondback."

Krups looked doubtfully at Cord hanging on to Heelkicker's neck with both hands, his legs dangling uselessly on the horse's flanks. "Why do I have to put up more money?"

Devlin consulted his watch again. "Because there's less than twenty seconds left. Did you expect the same odds?"

Cord's grasp on the stallion's neck was broken as Heelkicker twisted his great head. His body slipped toward the ground.

"Did you see that?" Krups said, his face breaking into a relieved smile. "Diamondback can't last another five seconds. My original bet stands. In fact, I'll sweeten it by another fifty dollars if you dare."

"I always dare," Devlin said. "And the man's a sentimental favorite. You have a bet."

As he slid helplessly down the horse's flank, Cord grasped the stallion's mane in both hands and righted himself. Heelkicker skidded and twisted about the corral in a frenzy to shake his rider.

Krups and Devlin stared relentlessly at the watch

Devlin held in his open palm, with Krups occasionally glancing up, wincing to see Cord still bouncing on Heelkicker's back. "Fall off," Krups said, almost praying.

"Time's up," Devlin shouted. "All debts are due and payable. Hey, Diamondback, you can dismount now."

That's wonderful, Cord thought, but how the hell do I get off without being killed? Pain permeated the arm and leg that had been smashed into the corral posts. The insides of his thighs and crotch felt as if they'd been repeatedly smashed with a sledgehammer. Cord felt consciousness slipping away. He wanted to slip off the horse and go to sleep. He could think of nothing more wonderful.

Heelkicker seemed to sense Cord's mood. He bucked in a series of short staccato moves that hit Cord as if a number of small rumbling earthquakes were rippling across the stallion's back. The ground's going to open up and swallow us both, Cord thought.

Heelkicker headed for the corral fence again, Cord hanging on tightly to the mane and ears, fearing the horse planned a repeat of his fence-smashing performance. About eight feet from the fence, the stallion leaped into the air, his front hooves at almost a seventy-five-degree angle from the ground. Cord felt the sweaty mane slipping through his hands as the stallion cleared the barrier with a jump that would have won him the English Derby. The horse bucked one final time, sending the nuisance on his back sailing. Heelkicker headed for the nearby hills.

Cord landed hard on his shoulder in the gravel

outside the corral, sliding for a few feet before skidding to a halt. Stones and pebbles dug into his back and side, scrubbing the skin off his forearm.

"You should work on your form." Devlin grinned.

"You've lost the best damn stallion this ranch ever had," Krups accused. "My hands will need at least two days to round him up again. I want you two men off this ranch, pronto."

"Of course," Devlin said. "We won't overstay our welcome. But first there's the matter of the hundred and fifty dollars you owe me."

"I only bet fifty."

"Ah, but we raised the bet twice in the heat of the moment."

"We did not."

"Don't be a welsher, Krups," Marty said. "Everyone here heard you raise the bets."

Krups glared at all three men as if unable to choose the one who had done him the most injury. "All right, I'll pay up. But both you slickers be away from this place in ten minutes." He turned and stalked toward the bunkhouse.

"We'll be gone the minute the money is in my palm," Devlin shouted after him.

Cord rose painfully, wiping off tiny trickles of blood from his skinned forearm. Every bone and muscle sent signals of protest to his brain, telling him never to do anything so foolish again. "Did you say something about a judging job?" he asked Devlin as he dusted himself off and inspected his torn shirt.

"I bring you proper employment just in the nick

of time," Devlin said. "You'd break your neck trying to ride these horses."

"What kind of judging does a gambler need?"

"None at all," Devlin protested. "I'm not the one who's hiring you. I recommended you to the disputing parties and was sent to fetch you."

"So you've no interest in the outcome?"

"A small one," Devlin admitted. "So remember me when you make your judgment. I'm entitled to some commission for getting you the job."

"Tell me the details," Cord asked. His bones still ached.

"I can't do that," Devlin said seriously. "I gave my word to the other people in this dispute. Everyone wants to be present when you're told the circumstances so you won't hear a version that favors any one participant."

"And they trusted you to bring me and keep your mouth shut? They must have been impressed by your honest Irish face."

"I said my stake is a small one," Devlin replied. His face lit up like the sun coming up over the horizon when he saw Krups returning with his money. "They didn't send me because I'm the most trustworthy man, only the one with the least to lose."

Krups counted out sticky greenbacks that had the look of having been buried in an old sock for years. "I don't want to see either of you men back here," he warned.

"You're five dollars short," Cord reminded Krups. "I rode that stallion."

"What? Heelkicker's taken off for far places because of you."

"I rode him," Cord persisted.

Krups counted out five more sticky greenbacks. "It's worth it to get rid of the two of you."

"If you can't tell me about the job, at least give me some information about the person doing the hiring," Cord said to Devlin as they rode away. "When do I get a chance to meet my employer?"

"You don't."

Cord reined his Appaloosa. "I'm not taking a judging job until I have a chance to meet my client," he protested. "We have to discuss the terms."

"The terms are already taken care of. I've negotiated a fine deal for you, Cord. You're getting five hundred dollars and you should be able to finish the job in two or three days."

"Not unless I meet the client," Cord said. "I'm not going into a job blind."

Devlin flashed Cord a big Irish grin. "Who said you couldn't meet him? Word of honor, I'll bring you to the man the minute we hit town. I only said you couldn't talk to him."

"Why can't I talk to him?"

"He's not a very interesting conversationalist," Devlin said, trying to hide a sly smile.

"Come on Devlin, make sense."

"I am, Bucko. Tim Brady's your employer. And you can't meet him because he's dead."

"Dead?"

Devlin turned toward Cord, no longer concealing his amusement. "Dead."

3.

"Do you remember that poker game in Sante Fe?" Devlin asked Cord as the ranch disappeared behind them.

"I should remember," Cord said. "You won almost every pot that night."

Devlin's grin disappeared as if he'd been wearing a wax face that melted in the sun. "Every pot but the biggest one. As I recall, Cord Diamondback walked away from the game with most of the money."

"You won too. Why does it bother you?"

"Because you're a damned amateur, and you beat me with a pair of sevens. A lousy pair of sevens!"

"You should have called," Cord reminded him. "Weren't you holding a low straight?"

"I don't announce the hands I throw away."

They rode in silence for ten minutes before Devlin started in again. "I know the cards, I play the odds, and I analyze the players," he grumbled. "I had my eye on you all night. You didn't make any mistakes, and you played well, but you didn't bluff once all night. Not once. I had you pegged as a solid player without the guts to run a bluff. Then, when the biggest pot of the night comes along, you threw all your holdings into the pot. With four hearts showing, what was I to think? I was sure you had a flush, so I folded. Deuce Devlin never throws good money after bad."

"That pot helped pay my way to New Orleans. Did I forget to thank you?"

"You had to turn up your cards. Did I ask to look at them? If I were that curious, I would have covered your bet. You didn't have your flush; you only held a small pair."

"You got some of your money back this afternoon," Cord said, reminded by his painful backside. "What made you bet on me, Devlin? You never make a wager unless the odds are in your favor."

"What makes a great artist?" Devlin asked unexpectedly.

Cord shrugged. He was in no mood for philosophical questions. "He sees something that most other people miss, I guess."

"The same quality makes a good gambler. Everyone at that ranch was hypnotized by that magnificent stallion. They saw him prancing and pawing and the fire in his eyes. The animal was an impressive sight to be sure. But while they were looking at him, I was looking at you. I saw the determination in your face. The look that said you wouldn't be beaten. That's why I bet on you, Bucko. You've got sand!"

Cord laughed. "Determination isn't enough of an edge for Deuce Devlin. How did you know I could stay atop that beast for a minute and a half?"

Devlin looked sideways at Cord with a tiny grin that suggested he knew a lot he wasn't saying. "You're a vain devil. What makes you think you stayed on that long?"

"Your watch, you timed it." Cord struck his forehead. "Deuce Devlin's watch."

Devlin smugly patted his watch pocket. "You were always quick, Diamondback. This watch is my little edge. The case says Bulova, but I had the works specially made in Switzerland. There's a tiny switch that makes time seem to move faster when I pull it forward. Back and time slows down. You'd be surprised at how many wagers revolve around a time limit."

Cord shook his head, still laughing. "I was convinced I stayed aboard Heelkicker for more than five minutes."

"You would have been up there a lot longer than five minutes if I had bet the other way."

Cord winced. "Tell me something about the town we're headed for," he said, anxious to change the subject.

"It's a small town called Los Gordos near Jesse Chisolm's spread in Lincoln County. There's a self-appointed sheriff in town by the name of Kane Richmond, but the closest official law comes out of Fort Sumner. The land all around the town is good cattle country. The Mexicans, who were the first settlers, named the place Los Gordos because the cattle who feed on the sweet grass become the 'fat ones.'"

Cord knew that Fort Sumner had been at the center of the Lincoln County wars. But the territorial governor, General Lew Wallace, had put an end to the killings long ago. The ranches were settled now and the rustling had stopped.

"I thought the land disputes were over," Cord said.

"Quit fishing," Devlin replied. "You'll learn why you've been hired after we get there." Cord had never known the gambler to be so tight-lipped.

"I remember the name Kane Richmond. Wasn't he considered a hot gun back a few years ago?"

Devlin nodded. "Still is from what I hear. He served as Pat Garrett's deputy during the time when things were really sticky in Fort Sumner. I understand he rode with Garrett over to Maxwell's place the night that Pat braced Billy Bonney. The town let him stay on as deputy even after Garrett lost the next election. Then one day Richmond had a few drinks too many and gunned down three men in a saloon because they were singing too loud. They almost hung him but settled for booting him out." Devlin turned in his saddle. "Stay away from him, Cord. He's dangerous and erratic. No telling what he'll do from one minute to the next."

"Why? I have a lovely singing voice."

4.

Four hot days and three chilly nights later, Cord and Devlin rode into Los Gordos and stabled their tired mounts at a rundown livery with the faded lettering BUCK'S ONE-BUCK STABLE, painted over the barn. As they had come down from the highlands, black thunderheads had rumbled at their backs but never quite caught up with them. The men had just walked out of the stable when the thick clouds delivered their promise, unleashing a torrent of rain on the town and travelers.

Cord and Devlin, their Stetsons pulled low over their faces, dashed through the dirt streets turning fast to mud as rain sloshed through the neck openings of their yellow slickers. They stomped on the raised wooden sidewalk, kicking caked mud from their boots, and shoved past the batwing doors of the General Lew Wallace Saloon.

Cord stopped just inside the entrance, peeled off his dripping slicker, and surveyed the place as he dried his wet face with his bandanna. The saloon walls, the floor, the steps leading to the second floor, even the bar were constructed of raw unfinished pine, as if whoever had built the place had given up three-quarters of the way through the job. At a back table, near a badly smoking wood stove, five men played faro. The men stopped their game to watch Cord and Devlin dry themselves off. Cord noticed another man slumped over a darkened table in a far corner. The man kept so still Cord thought he must be a drunk sleeping off a binge.

Thousands of past-spilled drinks stained the raw pine bar top. The whiskey had eaten into the raw wood, leaving the surface warped and uneven so it was impossible to rest a shot glass there without some tilt. Above the bar hung a circus poster of a plump female bareback rider dressed in pink tights that accented her fleshiness. She rode a black steed who seemed to be galloping right across the dusty bottles on the back shelf. Some deadeye had drilled neat .44 holes directly in the center of the rider's ample breasts, somehow adding to the eroticism of the picture.

The bartender, a handsome Mexican with white teeth that almost sparkled, flashed his smile at Cord and Devlin. He reached to the back shelf for a bottle of tequila, poured two generous glasses, and motioned to the newcomers.

"On a night like this, the first drink is on the house," the Mexican said without a trace of an accent. He poured a glass for himself and raised it. "A toast to the return of Mr. Devlin. He has obviously succeeded in his mission."

"Is this the judge?" one of the cardplayers asked. The player had a thin wrinkled face that screwed up in doubt when he looked at Cord.

"This is the famous Diamondback, gentlemen,"

Devlin replied, putting his hand on Cord's shoulder as if they were old friends. "Cord, how do you like the General Wallace? This is a fair sampling of the nightlife in Los Gordos."

"Comfy, real comfy."

"You were misguided to travel all the way to New Orleans for your pleasure," Devlin said. "Anything a man could possibly want is right here."

"Damn right," the faro player said, completely missing Devlin's sarcasm. "Hey, Deuce, how about sitting in on our game?"

"Not if you're still playing for the same piddling stakes."

"I guess it ain't fittin' to ask the judge to take a hand?" the faro player hopefully asked.

Cord ignored the question. "Who's the sharpshooter?" he asked, referring to the person who had hollowed out the bareback rider's nipples.

The bartender made a distasteful movement with his mouth. "That was our so-called sheriff, Kane Richmond. He got drunk one night and wanted to prove he could still handle a gun."

"If the sheriff shoots up the saloon, who keeps the peace?" Cord asked.

The bartender raised his shoulders in an eloquent Mexican shrug.

"Don't ask Felipe about Kane Richmond," Devlin said. "They ain't buddies."

Cord noticed the awful stench after he'd finished his first drink of tequila. The pinewood scent and the odor of stale beer partially masked the terrible smell, but it seemed to build until its foulness crowded out all other senses. Cord couldn't understand why the others weren't bothered because the stench was heavy and sour and somehow depressing. It started Cord's stomach churning. He'd smelled something like this once before aboard his ship when the second mate had gotten gangrene after accidentally being gaffed by a harpoon during a whaling run. The mate had kept quiet about his problem because he feared the captain might throw him overboard like fish offal. He'd let his foot fester and almost rot away before the smell revealed his secret. The captain ordered Cord to hold the screaming mate down while the leg was amputated with a knife used for cutting into whale blubber.

"You should air this place out once in a while," Cord told Felipe.

The Mexican's friendliness faded behind an impassive mask. "Sí, señor," he said, his flawless English disappearing.

"Don't blame Felipe," Cord heard a feminine voice say. "We're all so used to the stench nobody notices anymore."

Cord looked up quickly toward the flight of stairs leading to the saloon's second floor. Peering down from the balcony at the head of the stairs was a woman in her midthirties. Her green velvet dress covered a plush figure rivaling that of the bareback rider's. Her cheeks were plump and rosy and the tiniest trace of a double chin revealed she'd been eating well. She had light chestnut hair piled on top of her head with one tendril falling forward into her eye. She pushed the hair back onto her forehead with a smile that caused a dimple in her chubby cheek.

"Hello, Maribeth," Deuce Devlin called up the stairs. "I'd like you to meet Cord Diamondback."

Maribeth came clumping down the stairs, her high heels threatening the stability of the crude woodwork. She reached Cord, captured his arm, and presented her dimpled cheek to be kissed. "I've heard about you since I dealt in the gold fields above Sacramento. Always wanted to meet Cord Diamondback."

"And now that you've met me?"

Maribeth curtsied and affected a southern accent. "Thrilled that your honor will decide the final winner of the big poker game."

Cord turned to Devlin. "Is this big game the reason I'm here?"

"Maribeth's spilled the beans, Bucko," Devlin said. "This will be the easiest five hundred dollars you ever made. Just decide the winner of the last pot of the evening and walk off into the sunset, the richer for the experience."

"Were you one of the players?" Cord asked Maribeth.

"No, I was just the dealer," Maribeth said, pouting. "They wouldn't let me play."

"She can't get a seat in any heavy-stakes game," Devlin commented. "Her nimble fingers keep forgetting to deal from the top."

"Why, Mr. Devlin, how you do go on."

"Why use her as a dealer then?"

"Best dealer in the West as long as she's not involved in the game."

"Thank you, suh." Cord saw that Maribeth enjoyed clowning.

Cord looked from Maribeth to Devlin. He had a feeling that neither of them could be trusted. "In a poker game, the cards speak for themselves. Why do you need a judge when the cards can tell you who the winner is?''

"Well, you see it's like this. . . ." Devlin started.

"Careful, señor." Felipe had been listening carefully to the conversation and reached across the bar to put a warning hand on Devlin's shoulder.

"I forgot," Devlin said, brushing the Mexican's hand aside. "I promised not to say anything until everyone involved is present." Devlin turned his full Irish charm on the bartender. "Don't worry, Felipe, I haven't told him anything yet."

"Do you have a stake in this?" Cord asked Felipe.

"My sister was cheated out of her money."

"Come off it," Devlin said. "Corazón was in the game, but she didn't lose much."

"We do not expect justice at the hands of gringos," Felipe said, refilling Cord's glass as if he hoped he was wrong.

Cord considered what he'd learned. Maribeth wasn't one of the players, Devlin apparently hadn't lost much money, and Felipe seemed more concerned about his family's honor than anything else. "Seems to me if this was such a big game, I'm only talking to the fringe element. When do I get to meet the main players?"

"Tomorrow," Devlin said. "By now everyone knows you're in town and will show up here tomorrow. We'll tell you the complete story then."

"And my only job is to separate the winner from all the losers?"

Devlin and Felipe exchanged worried glances. "Not exactly," Devlin said, lighting up one of his cheroots. "The identity of the biggest loser is already widely known."

"How can that be? I haven't heard the details, and until I do, I won't make my judgment."

Devlin smiled and crooked a finger toward Cord. "This way."

"Oh for God's sake, Deuce," Maribeth cried. "Leave it for tomorrow."

Devlin turned toward Felipe. "You have any objections if I show him now?" The bartender shook his head. "This way," Devlin repeated.

Cord followed the gambler to a darkened corner where he had seen the drunk slumped over the table. The closer they got to the table, the stronger the stench, until Cord was forced to place a handkerchief over his mouth. Maribeth came to about fifteen feet from the table and pulled to a stop. Another few feet and Cord had moved close enough to see what caused the awful odor.

The man slumped over the table wasn't drunk. He was dead. The back of his head had been shot away, leaving a gaping hole that looked like the entrance to a forbidding cave. Two green flies, gorged to bursting with blood, sat preening their legs on the edge of the crusted wound and flew grudgingly away as Cord and Devlin approached. Cord could tell from the stiffness of the body and foulness of the smell that the man had been dead for at least six days, maybe more. He calculated that was just about the time it took for Deuce Devlin to find him and bring him back to Los Gordos.

"Meet your client, Tim Brady," Devlin said, blowing smoke in the corpse's face.

5.

"Why did you leave the body here?" Cord asked. "Aren't there any vacancies in your cemetery? I'd think you'd want to bury the man just to be rid of the smell."

"There was too much riding on the game to plant Brady right away," Devlin said. "When he goes under doesn't matter to him, but the outcome of the game means riches or poverty for some of the players. We took a vote and decided we wanted you to see everything just the way it was when the shooting happened."

"Who shot him?" Cord asked.

"Nobody knows," Maribeth said. "He was shot from a small outside window at the back of the saloon. The shot broke some window glass before hitting Brady's skull. Nobody saw anyone outside, so we only know who didn't shoot him."

"Obviously you mean the other players in the game," Cord said. He scanned the table setting. Brady's bloodless, stiffened hand lay across a mound of red, white, and blue poker chips as if the dead man's last act had been to rake in the pot. A dried trickle of blood, looking like a dried creek bed headed nowhere, meandered across the green felt table covering. Three official-looking documents, apparently legal papers, lay toward the center of the table, anchored by empty whiskey glasses. Discarded cards, all facedown, were scattered everywhere. A few of the cards were spattered with blood, making them appear to have been marked by a bad cheat. A half deck of undealt cards rested neatly on one end of the table far from the chips. Cord guessed that was where the dealer, Maribeth, sat. Five empty wooden chairs rested a few feet from the table as if the former occupants had pulled away from the action. On the table in front of two of the empty chairs, on a spot close to the corpse, lay four draw-poker hands. Ten-penny nails had been hammered into the center of each of the hands, securely fastening them to the surface.

"I can see nothing has been moved," Cord said. "I know you don't want to discuss this until tomorrow, but tell me who the other players were. They can be eliminated from suspicion for Brady's murder."

"It's not that simple," Devlin said. "Not all the players were still at the table when the shooting occurred. In that last hand, when the stakes got too high, those who dropped out of the pot either went home or left the room for some air."

"You mean people walked out without waiting to see the outcome of the night's biggest pot?" Cord shook his head in disbelief. "That goes against a gambler's instinct."

"What difference does that make?" Felipe exploded.

"Felipe's right," Devlin said. "You're not being paid to solve a murder case; you're here to judge the winner of a poker hand."

"Think about it tomorrow," Maribeth said. "I have some ideas about a private game for tonight."

Cord shrugged. He wouldn't push an investigation if the people who hired him didn't want one. Why complicate his job? But he felt it was important to know the identity of backshooters. The man or woman who killed Tim Brady from ambush might be an upstanding member of the community, like Senator Fallows. Whenever he thought about Fallows, the jagged scar tissue that branded him as a murderer and fugitive tingled. Cord had made the senator pay with his own life for killing his brother, and now he was a hunted man unable to use his own name. The experience hadn't turned him into an avenging angel; he was too busy surviving for that. But he did like to know who the backshooters were.

"We've told you too much already," Devlin said. "The others are likely to be angry if we spill any more. Let's finish this discussion tomorrow when everyone's here."

The batwing doors burst open, letting in a blast of cold wind that carried rain clear into the center of the saloon. Riding the rain into the room was a gaunt man, thin as a shadow, dressed in a poncho that didn't keep his pants from turning sopping wet below his knees. The man was hatless and the rain plastered his sparse black hair against his skull, making his lean, hollow face appear even thinner. A hawk nose, scarred but unbroken, started just below his colorless eyes and curved down his face until it seemed to touch narrow, bloodless lips. The man licked those lips nervously as his eyes studied Cord from head to foot like a hungry wolf eyeing a potential kill.

"Hello, Richmond," Devlin said. "What mission of the law brings you out on a night like this?"

"I heard the hired judge was in town," Richmond said, still sizing up Cord with his wolfish eyes. "I thought as one professional to another, it was only proper that I pay my respects."

Cord could see that Kane Richmond had already made up his mind to dislike him, maybe even hate him for some unknown reason. Not that Cord gave a damn how the man felt. But how Richmond planned to behave concerned him a great deal.

"I appreciate your getting wet on my account, Sheriff," Cord said, making his own appraisal. So this was the almost-famous gunslinger. Kane Richmond didn't have a big reputation, but he was feared by other professionals. Some said that Pat Garrett kept him on the payroll to bolster his own reputation. The man was supposed to be quick and accurate but skittish. When spooked, he'd gun down anyone standing in front of him. Since his top years in Fort Sumner, hair-trigger guns had gotten Richmond many a job keeping the peace, and hair-trigger nerves had lost them all.

"I come here to set you straight, Diamondback," Richmond said, continuing his dogged stare. "You're intruding on my territory in two ways and I don't like it. First, I'm the law in this town—"

"Self-appointed," Felipe interrupted.

The sheriff fixed his stare on Felipe. "My rates is cheap," he said. He turned to Cord. "I don't charge the folks anything to keep the peace except for taking a cut on the gambling in town. So having you waltz in here as a judge to settle a gambling argument is a personal insult. And I don't take insults. I thought I'd come here tonight and explain things. Give you a chance to leave town without any holes in your hide."

"I'm grateful for your thoughtfulness, Richmond. But if you're the sheriff and control the gambling, why did these folks send for me?"

"Because nobody trusts him," Felipe said. "He would have sold his decision to the highest bidder."

"Shut up, Mex," Richmond snarled. Cord noticed the way Richmond kept both hands hovering close to his twin Colt .45s. The guns' pearl handles still beaded with rain. If Richmond drew, would the slickly wet handles slow him down? Make him fumble? Cord decided he didn't want to find out.

"Thanks for telling me where you stand, Sheriff," Cord said. "Some of the people in this town hired me to do a job and I'll stay to do it."

"The famous Cord Diamondback." Richmond's voice dripped with sarcasm. "Messing in things that ain't none of your business. You ain't no proper judge and maybe you can't back up your decisions with your gun." Richmond's face turned from threatening to quizzical. "I ever see you before?"

"Could be," Cord replied. "I get around."

"Diamondback has done some boxing," Devlin volunteered. "Maybe you saw him in the ring."

The sheriff shook his head slowly. "That ain't it. I never seen a prizefight." He peered at Cord. "You ever been a peace officer?"

Cord shook his head slowly. "I couldn't stand the company I'd have to keep."

Maribeth tittered and Devlin's face creased into a big Irish smile. Even Felipe's mouth seemed to light up at the corners.

Richmond glared at the amused crowd and then at Cord. His pistols jumped into his hand. At least that's the way it seemed to Cord. One second the gun was in the man's holster, the next it appeared in his hand. That answers my question about his ability to handle a piece with a wet handle, Cord thought. No sense in trying to clear leather now. With Richmond's twin Colts pointed straight at his chest, it would be suicide.

"You can't shoot him in cold blood," Maribeth cried.

"There are too many witnesses here, Richmond," Cord said. "Or do you plan to shoot them all too?"

"Hey, stop giving the man ideas," Devlin protested.

"Who said anything about shooting anyone?" Richmond said, a smug, satisfied look on his face. "The place where I saw your face just came back to me, and it wasn't in any book on peace officers. It was on a wanted poster issued out of San Francisco. I don't remember the name on the poster, but it wasn't Cord Diamondback. There's a reward on your head, mister, and I'm hauling your ass to jail."

6.

"You couldn't find anything, could you?" the voice shouted from the other room. "Not one thing."

Cord came awake shivering under the thin cotton blanket provided by the sheriff. The skin on his back prickled from the straw poking through the dirty muslin cover of the worn mattress. He hoped that was the only reason he was itching. His first night under a roof in four days and it had to be in the cold comfort of an adobe jailhouse. The loud voices in the other room weren't helping him sleep and he needed rest to think his way out of this mess.

What time was it? Cord glanced through the single barred window at the steady rain pelting out of the night sky. Still nowhere near morning. Who the hell was out there in the sheriff's office kicking up such a fuss in the middle of the night? Fully awake now, he concentrated on the loud but muffled sounds drifting through the wooden jailhouse door.

"You went through every poster for the past five years and you didn't find one on Cord Diamondback, did you?" That voice definitely belonged to a woman. Cord didn't recognize her, but she sounded

43

young and angry. Good. Anyone who was indignant about his incarceration had to be all right.

"That don't mean he's not wanted. Not by a long shot it don't." Ah, that was the so-called sheriff, Kane Richmond. His voice carried an unfamiliar defensive tone. Could it be that the famous gunfighter wasn't holding his own against this female?

"You have nothing to hold him on and the law says you must let him go." Cord smiled to himself. Unfortunately men like Richmond paid little attention to what the law said.

"My stock of wanted posters ain't complete," the sheriff complained. "The government don't send them to me because I ain't an official peace officer. But I seen that man's picture someplace and dollar signs was under it. No matter what you say, I'm holding him right here until I get a chance to ride to Fort Sumner and go through their old files."

"You can't keep a man locked up on unfounded suspicion." The woman's voice sounded like she was used to ordering people about. "I'm telling you to release him."

"Your orders don't mean anything to me." Cord recognized Richmond's old snarl. "Just wait," the sheriff continued. "When I come back from Fort Sumner, I'll have the goods on him." Wait a minute! Richmond had called the young woman "Miss Brady." He must be speaking to Tim Brady's daughter. Why hadn't Devlin told him the dead man had a family?

"Just let him out until you get back," the woman persisted. "If you find any outstanding warrants in Fort Sumner, arrest him again when you return."

Richmond laughed, a dry gunman's laugh without feeling behind it. "If there's a bounty on him, you think he'd be here when I got back? I'd be throwing the reward money away."

"So it's money you're after," the woman said scornfully.

Hell, *I'd* even like the reward money, Cord thought. You must be young, Miss Brady, if the idea of greed comes as a revelation.

"I want the reward, sure," Richmond said, "but I been a peace officer too long to watch wanted criminals walk around." Bull! Cord thought. He's negotiating.

"What if I posted twenty-five hundred dollars' bail on this man?" Brady's daughter asked. "That's more than most rewards, isn't it? If you find a wanted poster on Diamondback and lose the bounty because he's left town, I forfeit the bail. You get paid whether he's here or not." Miss Brady, you just took the bait, Cord thought.

"What if there's a poster on him, but the bounty's less than twenty-five hundred?" Richmond's voice had a crafty ring, like a merchant offering a puny discount on overpriced goods.

"Keep the whole thing!" the woman cried. Cord was beginning to feel affection for Tim Brady's foolish daughter, sight unseen.

Cord heard an iron key clanking in the door lock. Money had persuaded the sheriff. Cord arose from his smelly cot anxious for the first look at his benefactor.

Richmond walked through the door first, his skinny body obscuring Cord's view of Brady's daughter. He realized she was tall because he caught sight of sandy hair, the same tawny hue as a lion's coat, bobbing above the sheriff's head. She waited until Richmond had stepped into the cell, then posed in the doorframe for a moment before sweeping into the room with regal splendor. She was young all right, maybe twenty-one or twenty-two. She wore her long hair loose, letting it tumble down her back until it rested and curled on her shoulders. Her wide dark eyes inspected Cord from beneath dark lashes, in startling contrast to her fair, almost creamy complexion. Her mouth was a glossy pink bow currently turned down in a petulant frown. Her body was slim but delicately curved, promising to develop into ripe beauty as she matured. Her legs were clad in jodhpurs with glistening leather boots rising to her knees. A fitted silk blouse was tucked into the pants, and she folded her slender arms around her slim breasts as if trying to keep out the chill. She had a look of stunning, almost careless beauty combined with youthful innocence. Cord felt eager to hear her speak, prepared to like anything she had to say.

"I can see you're not going to be much help." Her wide eyes colored in disdain as they studied Cord. Her pert nose wrinkled in disgust as she looked around the cell and spotted the chamberpot. "What kind of a judge has to be bailed out of jail his first night in town?"

"A judge who isn't quicker on the draw than a notorious gunslinger," Cord replied. Out of the corner of his eye he noticed Richmond scowl at his remark. "I take it you're Tim Brady's daughter?"

"Yes," she said, eyeing Cord skeptically. "I'm Rosalyn Brady." She shook her head emphatical. "I just can't believe you're really a judge. If you weren't representing my late father in that ridiculous poker game, I'd have let you rot in this pigsty."

"I'm getting all the details tomorrow," Cord said. "Will you be there?"

Rosalyn Brady's eyes burned angrily. "I suppose the meeting will be in the saloon where they're holding my father's body. What they're doing in this town isn't right, Mr. Diamondback. My father deserves a decent funeral and I want you to see that he gets it. When that's done, I need your help in getting his rightful winnings out of that pot."

"Excuse me, Miss Brady," Cord said. "I understand that you're concerned about burying your father and I think the others will agree to it now that I'm in town. But I'm a judge, not a lawyer. I'm here to pick the winner of a disputed hand, not represent any single interest."

"Oh, that's a technicality," she said, exasperated. "I'm the one paying your salary and you'll do what I say." Rosalyn Brady threw her hands toward the ceiling as if she was trying to pull divine guidance down from the heavens. "God, how I hate this uncivilized place. The only way I can get what's rightfully mine is by using a phony judge who turns out to be a jailbird."

Cord smiled. "Something tells me you're new to the West."

Rosalyn Brady looked at Cord as if the place and manner of her upbringing would be obvious to all but the crudest of persons. "There are no decent schools here so my father sent me to Europe for my education. I've only been back a few weeks, and now he's been murdered. I mourn my father, but I can't wait for *mon retour dans la belle France*. The West is so . . ." She let the sentence hang as if no word was harsh enough.

Cord frowned. His initial positive reaction to Tim Brady's daughter didn't survive their first minute together. She seemed a typical rich man's spoiled offspring. Just one whiff of European culture and she felt she had soared high above her father's humble beginnings. Still, she had gotten him out of jail and for that Cord was grateful. "You're right, Miss Brady, we do many things differently out here. I can understand your desire to return to France."

Her dark eyes flickered in surprise. "A cowboy who understands French? Is there more to you than meets my eye, Mr. Diamondback?"

"Whenever you two stop talking you can get out of my jail," Richmond said. "I'm turning you loose, Diamondback. Go where you like. I don't give a damn." Richmond kept his voice casual. "I'm thinking of, uh, taking a few days off."

"I'll miss you, Richmond," Cord said. "You brighten up the place." Cord pretended he hadn't overheard the earlier conversation between Richmond and the girl. He wondered what the sheriff would find in Fort Sumner. How far back did they keep their wanted posters? When Richmond left town, maybe he should ride fast in the opposite direction, put plenty of miles between them. But what if the sheriff uncovered the old posters on Christopher Deacon and recognized Cord Diamondback? The identity and reputation he had carefully built up over the past half-dozen years would be destroyed. Where could he go? Even if the sheriff came up empty, the news that Diamondback had run away when someone started checking on him would spread like a herd of cattle stampeding before a prairie fire. Sheriffs and bounty hunters all over the West would be digging up old posters, poking through yellowed files. Sooner or later someone would put the pieces together. My best option is staying right here, Cord thought. Maybe Richmond won't find anything. Meantime, I'd better work a plan in case the sheriff gets lucky.

Cord barely heard Rosalyn Brady's voice above the wind as they hustled back to the General Lew Wallace Saloon, leaning against the driving rain. "I just want to give my father a funeral and sell the ranch so I can return to Paris. My fiancé is waiting for me. I'm marrying a count," she said proudly. *"Il est d'une lignée illustre."*

A sudden gust of harsh wind destroyed her umbrella, tearing off the cloth and sending it sailing down the muddy street. She kept the ribbed skeleton above her head as the rain poured down on her. Cord thought she deserved a soaking. Anyone who bragged about her intended's illustrious heritage during a rainstorm was all wet to begin with.

"Do you have interested buyers for the ranch?" Cord asked.

"The place hasn't been put up for sale."

"Why not? Is there a problem with your father's estate?"

"There's one gigantic problem," Rosalyn shouted to make herself heard over the wind. "Everything my father owned is tied up in that stupid poker game."

Cord stopped to walk around a street puddle that was beginning to acquire the dimensions of Mammoth Lake. "Your father bet his *ranch* on the poker hand?"

"He had the winning cards all right," Rosalyn said. "I'm absolutely sure of it. Daddy gambled, but he wasn't a plunger unless he had a sure thing. That's probably why he was killed. Well, my father bet and he won. That poker hand, everything in that pot, is part of my inheritance. I want a clear deed to the ranch so I can sell it, and I want everything else that's on that table. It's all mine."

Cord remembered seeing legal documents on the grisly poker table. "If your father put up his ranch, the other players must have anted something of equal value to stay in the pot."

"We're not supposed to tell you until tomorrow, but there's no harm in you knowing because the money belongs to me anyway. Jake Langely, he's another rancher, put up a bill of sale on a herd of five thousand cattle. Sam Buck, who owns just about everything in town, including the saloon, put up the stock in his freight line." She laughed girlishly. "I'm bringing quite a dowry to my Alfred. He's the count. It's a good thing because his family doesn't have a penny."

The streets had become a morass threatening to suck off their boots and perhaps swallow them as well with every step they took. Cord noticed that Rosalyn attacked the mud resolutely, moving firmly ahead, apparently not caring if she soiled her jodhpurs. They struggled onto the wooden sidewalk and under the comparative shelter of a roof overhang. Cord stopped Rosalyn just outside the saloon.

"How can you be absolutely sure your father held the winning hand? It appears to me as if all the cards were nailed to the table before anyone looked at them."

"I told you," she said, speaking slowly as if to a child. "My daddy would never have bet his ranch unless he had a hand that couldn't be beat."

Rosalyn's remark carried into the General Wallace, and Felipe eyed them both with hostility as they entered. "There was to be no explanation or discussion until tomorrow when we are all present," he said, his flawless English returning. Except for Felipe, the room was empty.

"No advantage gained, Felipe, I assure you." Cord yawned. "Do you have a hotel in this town? Maybe I can salvage a few hours' sleep before the meeting tomorrow."

"There's a room reserved for you upstairs," Felipe said. "Compliments of Mr. Sam Buck."

Rosalyn huddled near Cord, who noticed that she avoided looking toward the far corner where her father's corpse moldered. "Let me come upstairs with you for a minute," she said, shivering. "I have much more to tell you."

"The gringos conspire together," Felipe said bitterly. "Mr. Devlin goes to fetch you; Mr. Buck gives you a free room. Who knows what delights the señorita plans to offer the distinguished judge?"

"That's an awful thought," Rosalyn cried. "You're just a dirty-minded Mexican. I have every right to discuss the situation because I'm paying him and I bailed him out of jail."

"Let it wait until tomorrow," Cord said wearily. "I'm very tired and it's obvious that some of the other claimants would be concerned if you told your story before they have a chance to tell theirs."

"Do not misinterpret me, señor," Felipe said, his handsome face breaking into a wry grin. "By all means have a private meeting with the señorita in your room. Take as long as you like. The results could be very interesting."

"See, he doesn't mind," Rosalyn said in a stage whisper. "This is so very important and I'll only take a minute."

"One minute and that's all," Cord said, his eyes drooping. "And this had better be damn vital."

Cord started up the stairs with Rosalyn trailing behind. She had almost reached the second-floor landing when she stopped. "Can I trust you not to try anything, you know . . . nasty?"

"Tonight you can," Cord said, stifling another yawn.

"Sí, señorita," Felipe called up to them. "Tonight Señor Diamondback is a very trustworthy man."

How the hell would you know? Cord thought as he opened the door to his room. Rosalyn Brady swept past him, stopped still, put her hands to her face, and screamed. *Quelle horreur!*

7.

"I assumed that you'd come alone," Maribeth Adams said, rising from the small table set with a bottle of champagne and a deck of playing cards. "But I should have known it wouldn't take Cord Diamondback long to find another woman."

Maribeth's lush figure was only partially concealed by a blue velvet robe buttoned low at the top so the valley between her breasts beckoned like the promised land. The robe parted just below her thighs, revealing firm shapely legs encased in shocking-red silk stockings. The robe snugly fitted Maribeth's every curve. She obviously wore nothing beneath. In a small fireplace at the far end of the room, two pine logs burned lustily, backlighting Maribeth's dyed red hair with a rosy glow. The flickering flames deepened the fleshy tones of Maribeth's bare skin, combining with the red silk stockings to give her a warm, almost smoldering look.

Rosalyn Brady appeared scandalized as she took in the scene. "I bailed you out of jail so you could wallow in depravity with this woman?" she asked. "I've never seen anything so disgusting."

"This isn't nearly as disgusting as the cell I just left," Cord said. "But I really didn't know that Maribeth would be here."

"Oh, if you thought about it, you might have guessed," Maribeth said, obviously relishing the situation. "I gave you plenty of hints when you were in the saloon earlier."

"So you knew!" Rosalyn said. She appeared to be groping for a French word to cover her feelings. Finding none, she continued. "And you let me come up to your room to flaunt your conquest. What kind of justice can I expect from such a depraved judge?"

"A few minutes earlier you sounded like you were trying to influence my decision," Cord said. "What did you hope to gain by coming up here? What kind of justice did you want?"

"The two things are different; anyone can see that." Rosalyn's eyes swept around the room, drinking in every detail, probably storing up a tale of the loose ways in the primitive West to relate to her cultured European friends. "I'm obviously in the way here. Good night, Mr. Diamondback. Forgive me if I don't wish you a pleasant evening."

"I'll do that for you, dearie," Maribeth said with a broad grin.

Rosalyn opened the door and stood for an instant in the frame. "Barbarians!" she said, and slammed the door after her.

"What's with her?" Maribeth said, putting her arms around Cord. "Doesn't she think men and women get together in Europe?"

"I don't know what she thinks," Cord said. "And I don't know what you think is going to happen tonight, but I just want a night's sleep. I'm dead tired."

"Not one little hand of cards where the winner gets to tell the loser what to do?" Maribeth pouted.

Cord smiled. "Not with your reputation for slick dealing." He put his hand on the mattress. It felt soft and inviting. "I'm sorry, Maribeth, I'm going to turn in . . . alone."

"Cord, you sound as cold as the champagne," Maribeth complained. She stood close to him so that her breasts touched his forearm. He could smell the heavy rose scent she had applied to each nipple.

"I wouldn't do that wonderful body of yours justice tonight." Cord took her arm and started to lead her to the door. "Some other time."

Maribeth burst out laughing. "You can't kick me out. This is my room."

"Apparently Felipe made a mistake," Cord said. "I'll get another room."

"You can't. Everything else is taken. Even Devlin is doubling up."

"Maybe Richmond thought he was doing me a favor by putting me in jail," Cord said dryly.

"Stay here with me," Maribeth pleaded.

"I really need some rest." Cord's eyelids seemed to weigh a ton.

"Oh, get your precious sleep," Maribeth said petulantly. "If you stay here, I won't bother you. I promise to be a perfect lady all night."

"Do you mean it?" Cord sounded doubtful.

"On my honor as a dealer."

"I've heard what that's worth." Cord laughed.

The room's double bed supported a goose-down mattress covered with soft cotton ticking. Cord removed his boots and pants, carefully retaining his shirt, and sunk into the mattress, dozing off almost as soon as he pulled the crazy-quilt comforter over his body. Through half-closed eyes he saw Maribeth remove her robe and slip into bed next to him, naked except for her thigh-length red silk stockings. "I don't care how tired you are," he thought he heard her say as he went under. "You can take off that damn shirt."

The sun's first light caught Cord's eyes and pried under his eyelids. Raw harsh light flashed onto his retinas as the eyelids fluttered open. He blinked rapidly as another more pleasurable sensation swept over him. He brought his eyes into focus and looked down toward the foot of the bed. The crazy-quilt mattress had been swept to the floor, exposing Cord's lean muscled body. Maribeth's hand grasped the base of his penis, her mouth less than inches away as she tongue-flicked along the length of the shaft like an anteater after a really big colony.

She glanced up toward his face when she saw his eyes were open. "I only promised to behave last night," she said, her hand still moving on his penis. "The sun's been up for more than an hour."

Her naked body sprawled across Cord's legs with her fleshy soft breasts rubbing his thighs close to his ball sac. Her tongue moved rapidly across the head of his penis, her hazel eyes widening in wonder as it stiffened.

"That's the Cord I wanted," she said, taking the head of his penis into her mouth. He felt the warm wetness envelope him as her tongue played with the tip, gently batting it from cheek to cheek like a shuttlecock.

Cord thought he could be fond of Maribeth but wouldn't risk being in the same poker game with her. He reached his hand toward the foot of the bed and stroked the back of her head as she took more of his penis into her mouth. He felt her teeth gently scraping the sides as she swallowed his length.

Cord watched his penis disappear beyond her lips, then reappear glistening with saliva. Each time it reappeared, he could see traces of her bright red lipstick all around the shaft. Maribeth burrowed her body between his legs, reaching up her hands and cupping his ass cheeks. Her hands on his ass squeezed and kneaded as her head bobbed up and down. Cord felt his penis was being plunged in and out of a sticky honey jar. His semen started surging as Maribeth moved her head faster and faster. Maribeth sensed his orgasm and pushed his crotch into her face until her red bow lips were actually touching his pubic hair. Her fingers on his ass cheeks edged closer to his anus. Cord thrust his hips toward her plunging head, driving his penis farther down her throat. His semen bubbled to the surface like an underground geyser blowing off steam right on schedule. He snapped his hips into one great thrust as the semen spurted out the tip of his shaft and down her throat. Maribeth gave out a small cry of triumph as she swallowed the hot liquid and sucked him dry.

"Now, it's my turn," Maribeth said, seating herself on Cord's chest. Her black pubic patch winked at him only a few inches from his face. She still wore her red silk stockings, her legs straddling his torso. Cord's hands played with her voluminous breasts, which jutted out straight and proud as her large brown nipples grew hard as chestnuts from Cord's teasing. "Nice, oh that's so nice," she said, inching her body further up Cord's chest until her vagina brushed his lips. Cord kissed her vagina tenderly, pushing his tongue past her pubic hair and smelling her musky woman's smell, something like freshly turned earth. She reached her hands around the back of his neck and urgently pulled his mouth into her loins.

Cord's tongue explored her vagina lips, penetrating past the surface into the soft wet channel beneath. Maribeth gasped with pleasure as Cord's tongue moved around inside her. Her body moved on his face, grinding down until his chin and cheeks were slick with her juices. He could feel the cool satiny texture of her red silk stockings on his face as her knees pressed down alongside his head.

Cord felt his penis rising again as Maribeth thrashed wildly on his mouth. She reached one hand behind her, grasping his shaft as if she had hold of the reins on a runaway stallion. She tilted her body back to give Cord's mouth greater access to the full length of her sex. Cord felt the inside of her body pulsating as small gasps of animal pleasure came from her throat. Her hand pumped wildly on his penis as if she were willing him into an orgasm to match her own. Cord felt her clitoris flutter across his tongue like a moth attracted to a dangerous flame. He bucked his hips into her hand as she squirmed uncontrollably on his face. His semen squirted out the tip of his penis, covering her fist with a thick rich hand cream.

"My God, that was good," Maribeth said as they lay together, one of her stockinged legs sprawled across Cord's chest. "I'm just wondering how great a lover you could be if you ever took off your shirt and really got down to work."

"I'm saving that for the woman I marry," Cord said, smiling. He never met anyone he trusted enough to expose the mass of scars on his back. The wounds that had been carved into his hide so many years ago in San Francisco when he tried to save his brother had healed in the crude geometric pattern of a diamondback rattler. Every wanted poster on Christopher Deacon, killer of beloved Senator Fallows, described the scars in detail. None told the tale of why Cord was justified to do what he did.

"Is that a proposal?" Maribeth asked, breaking his reverie. "If it is, my answer is yes."

Cord laughed. "A husband would only get in your way, Maribeth."

Maribeth stroked his thigh with her open hand. "Seriously, Cord, why don't we team up for a while? I'm not talking about anything permanent, I know myself too well for that. But you have a reputation for honesty that we could cash like money in the bank. I deal in some high-stakes games, and you're a decent-enough poker player. Not as good as Devlin, mind, but you can hold your own with the professionals, especially if I were slipping you the right cards every now and then. No outrageous cheating, you understand. Just a little helping hand whenever the pot got juicy."

"You mean travel together? Go from town to town playing in big games?"

"Yeah," Maribeth said enthusiastically. "We'd

go where the money was. The traveling together, the celebrations, the champagne, the nights after a big score, that would be the fun part.''

"Don't you think folks would get suspicious when I collected aces all evening and later they saw us going into the same room?"

"Separate rooms?" she asked hopefully.

"Then what's the point?"

"I suppose you're right." She sighed. The fire had banked low and they both snuggled under the comforter with Maribeth's bare breasts nestled on Cord's arm. "You wouldn't have gone for it anyway, would you?"

"Gambling's not my profession. And crooked gambling is just too dangerous for me."

Maribeth giggled, not at all offended. "It's done all right by me."

"Tell me something about the poker game the night Tim Brady was killed," Cord asked, changing the subject. He felt warm and drowsy under the comforter as his hand stroked her generous bottom in a steady, soothing rhythm.

"Everybody promised not to tell you anything until we were all together." She arched her backside to meet his persistent hand. "Cord, if you don't stop doing that, you'd better be prepared to accept the consequences."

"You can tell me," Cord said. "From what I understand, you were the only participant who didn't have any interest in the outcome."

"That's right," Maribeth replied. Her breathing started coming in short gasps. "I was paid to serve as the dealer."

"Who hired you?" Cord asked. "How does the

premier dealer west of the Mississippi find a game in a town like Los Gordos. For that matter, how did Deuce Devlin get here?''

"Sam Buck sent for the both of us. I was in Taos running a game for miners who were working the silver claims. He offered me a hundred and fifty dollars to deal for just that one evening. I don't know where he found Deuce.''

"Felipe said my room was courtesy of Sam Buck,'' Cord recalled. "I'm sure I saw his name over the livery stable too.''

"Sam owns everything in town above the line that separates the Americans from the Mexicans,'' Maribeth said. "The bank, the freight line, everything. The ranchers around here really depend on him to keep the town going.''

"How did Sam know it was going to be a big-stakes poker game that required a professional dealer? Don't the stakes depend on all the players?''

Maribeth reached her hand down to Cord's ball sac and gently rolled his testicles in her hand like she was clacking a pair of dice. "If you're going to bother me, I'm going to bother you,'' she said. "How did Sam know? He told me that two ranchers in the area had challenged him to a high-stakes poker game. He said he was willing to sit in the game but didn't know cards well enough to recognize if anyone was cheating. He hired me to deal and Devlin to sit in the game because he figured between the two of us we'd be able to spot anything funny.''

"So you never met anyone before the game that night, including Sam Buck?'' Cord's penis began to lengthen under Maribeth's constant attention. She looked into his eyes and smiled.

"Sam sent for me by messenger," Maribeth said. "I never laid eyes on him until the night of the game."

"Who were the other players besides Sam Buck, Deuce Devlin, and Tim Brady?" Cord asked. Maribeth spread her legs as he massaged her bottom, allowing his probing hand to move lower and lower.

"Oh, the players, let me see." Maribeth started to squirm. "Corazón Lopez played in the game. She's Felipe's sister and the Mexican equivalent of Sam Buck in this town. For every piece of property Sam owns above the line, Corazón has a deed on something similar below the line. Apparently selling goods to the Mexicans is profitable. From what I hear, she's the richest lady in these parts."

"And the other player?"

"Longhorn Jake Langely. He's one of the original settlers of this section along with Jesse Chisolm and some others. Longhorn has the biggest spread in New Mexico next to Tim Brady's place. With Brady gone, I guess Langely's the biggest." Under Maribeth's steady stroking of his testicles, Cord's penis stretched and turned fleshy-purple as blood rushed into the area. His skin was prickly with heat, but he had to hold on until he got the information he wanted.

"Who else was there?"

"The usual hangers-on who stand around any big game. Kane Richmond was there making sure he'd collect his cut for allowing the game. And Corazón has an ox of a bodyguard who follows her around wherever she goes. I think his name is Sebastian, but I'm not sure because he never says a word."

"What was Richmond offering for his percentage?"

"Protection. With all that money in the game, Richmond said he'd make sure we weren't held up."

"He didn't protect Brady, did he?"

Maribeth shook her head slowly, more intent on what her hands were doing than the conversation.

"Tell me about the game itself."

"At first I was disappointed because the betting started small." She moved her hand from Cord's testicle to his hard penis. "Occasionally Deuce would run a bluff and win a small hand, but everyone at the table played conservatively." She looked up into his face with a smile. "The rest of the story will have to wait. There's an urgent matter in front of me right now."

The room door shook and splintering wood sounded like the crack of a nearby rifle. Cord glanced over, knowing he had locked it before turning in with Maribeth the previous evening. Locking doors was a natural precaution for him now. He scrambled out from under Maribeth's naked body as the door gave way, hinges and all, slamming with a loud crash that raised dust from the wooden floor.

8.

An ox in the shape of a man came crashing to the floor along with the door. An olive-skinned woman with jet-black hair swept back into a severe ponytail and high cheekbones that suggested some Indian ancestry followed the fallen giant into the room. Maribeth screamed and wrapped the comforter around her body as Cord leaped off the bed toward his Smith & Wesson Schofield.

"My brother, Felipe, was right," the woman said scornfully. "The gringo judge sleeps with the *puta* who dealt the cards that night. What justice can I expect?" She looked over to the powerful giant who had risen slowly and watched Cord warily as he rubbed his shoulder. "Sebastian, show the people of the town what the gringos are like. Throw this man of justice out the window."

Cord looked toward the bedpost where he always hung his gun and holster before retiring. The damn thing wasn't there! Maribeth must have put it some place else during the night while he slept. She should have known better—unless this was a setup. Sebastian advanced slowly, his huge gnarled hands opening and closing like bear traps. The Mexican stood a head taller than Cord and weighed a good hundred pounds more. His dark leathery head seemed a solid rectangle set on a square beam. He moved slowly, but Cord knew he had no room to maneuver within the confines of the tiny room. If only he had his pants on, he wouldn't feel so completely vulnerable. At least the intrusion had taken care of his erection. He kicked a chair in front of Sebastian, who stumbled, allowing Cord to rip a right cross to his chin.

"Can't we talk about this for a minute," Cord asked the woman as Sebastian shook his head, trying to clear it. "If you're Corazón Lopez, throwing me out the window sure isn't going to better your chances of recovering your losses."

"Talk as much as you like to Sebastian," the woman said. Her eyes showed the tiniest tinge of admiration as she took in Cord's lean muscled frame, completely naked from the waist down. "Perhaps he will listen to you, gringo."

Cord realized he'd wasted a precious advantage when the giant recovered and came at him again. Still too much the eastern lawyer, he thought. I'm still trying to talk my way out of situations when action is the only solution.

Cord kept the small card table between him and Sebastian. The Mexican's long arms, knotted like the branches on a giant sequoia, couldn't quite reach across; his wide swipes swept by Cord's face inches short. Sebastian moved ponderously, but Cord realized that in this small room he was sure to reach him sooner or later.

Cord feinted a move to his right, shifted left, and

hit Sebastian with a left hook to the nose. Blood spurted from the giant's nostrils and leaked across his mouth and down his chin. His pupils narrowed into red pin dots as he swept the table aside with one hand.

Cord feinted again, spinning behind the Mexican and thudding a fist into the nape of his neck. The blow landed with a thunk that would have felled a mule. Sebastian roared as he turned and charged, knocking Cord backward into Corazón Lopez. They both tumbled to the floor, Cord even more aware that he was naked from the waist down as he landed on top of her. As he fought to extricate himself from the tangle of limbs, he realized how soft and totally feminine she was. Her body smelled darkly exotic, like flowers from a tropical jungle.

"Excuse me," Cord said, scrambling to his feet.

"Por nada," she replied.

Sebastian advanced slowly, backing Cord into a corner of the small room. Cord feinted twice, but the giant didn't react so Cord put his head down and rushed the Mexican, ramming his skull into Sebastian's breadbasket. The Mexican's middle sagged like a cake taken out of the oven too soon. Cord swung a series of lefts and rights that sent the winded giant reeling. He stagged backward, Cord following quickly and landing blows at any spot left uncovered. Sebastian fell to one knee and Cord closed in for the kill, hammering fists to the giant's bloody face.

Blinded by blood seeping into his eyes, Sebastian swept his long arms in a circular motion, like a lumberjack cutting down a large pine with a long saw. His hand caught Cord by the ankle, upending him, and Cord hit the wooden floor hard. Sebastian advanced on his knees toward the fallen Diamondback. His gnarled hands wrapped completely around Cord's neck with inches to spare. He pushed his palms together as Cord grasped the giant's arms, trying to pry them apart. He felt the Mexican's muscles, hard as anthracite, and realized he had little chance against the brute's strength. Sebastian placed one knee on Cord's chest, pinning him to the floor. His hands tightened slowly, choking the life out of Diamondback.

Cord felt his windpipe being crushed, the pain forced up into his head until it seemed like the top of his skull would blow out from the pressure. He moved his hands up to Sebastian's face, trying for the Mexican's eyes, but they were out of reach. He kicked up with his feet, but Sebastian knocked his legs aside as if he were swatting a tiny flea.

Cord's vision blurred and he gasped for air as Sebastian increased the pressure. The pain disappeared for a moment and he realized he'd blacked out temporarily. I can't allow that to happen again, he thought. The next time will be my last. Concentrate on the pain. Use that to stay alive. He thumped his open palm into the Mexican's chin and the giant loosened his grip for one precious second, allowing Cord to take one greedy gulp of air. Damn! The air forced through his raw windpipe like emery dust.

Cord pried two of the Mexican's fingers apart, forcing one of the giant's hands off his throat. Sebastian shifted his other hand to the center and pushed down hard, squeezing Cord's Adam's apple into his windpipe.

Maribeth Adams trembled on the bed, clutching

the comforter around her naked body. Cord motioned to her frantically. "Hey, Sebastian," she called, lowering the blanket to her waist and letting her luscious breasts bob free.

The Mexican's head snapped up in surprise, his leering gaze lingering longer than it should have over her seminude body. His grip unconsciously lightened on Cord's body. Cord's hand swept the floor for a weapon. His fingers grasped something smooth and hard, the champagne bottle Maribeth had sitting on the card table last evening. It must have fallen to the floor when Sebastian knocked over the table. I'm glad that it's still full, Cord thought. When something was christened—like the bow of a ship or the thick skull of an opponent— tradition required the use of a full bottle of the bubbly.

Cord swung the champagne in a smooth arc, shattering the glass across the giant's temple. The exploding bottle sounded like a rifle shot as the sparkling wine sprayed across the room. The liquid soaked Corazón's blouse, making the silky fabric cling to her shapely breasts and misting in tiny beads in her black hair. Somehow she seemed more erotic than the still-naked Maribeth. Sebastian toppled to the floor. He rose slowly, holding his bleeding head and staggering about the room. Cord pushed the reeling giant toward the open window.

"Please no, señor," Corazón begged, wine streaming down her face. "You have finished him. We are on the second floor and a fall from this height could kill him."

"Seems to me we're on the same floor we were

on a few minutes ago. You didn't seem too concerned about that distance then."

"But you can afford to be generous, Señor Diamondback," Corazón Lopez protested.

"Sure," Cord said. He centered the semiconscious Sebastian against the window, sent three punishing left hooks to his midsection, doubling the Mexican over, and smashed a roundhouse right to his chin. Sebastian crashed through the window glass, tumbling head over heels down the second-floor overhang and thudding like an unexploded cannonball into the still-muddy street.

Corazón Lopez and Maribeth Adams came running to join Cord at the shattered window to view the small mud-walled crater created by Sebastian's body. Citizens of Los Gordos hustled toward the spot because they had thought the storm was over and here it was raining giants. A hand and then a head appeared from the crater's depths like slowly flowing lava from a newly formed volcano. The people below peered upward to Cord, Maribeth, and Corazón. Cord realized he was still naked below the waist and retreated back into the room.

"That was not necessary, señor," Corazón reproved. "You had beaten the man into submission."

"I gave him what you recommended for me," Cord reminded her as he hitched on his trousers. He felt more at ease now that he wasn't half naked.

"Perhaps I reacted too strongly when I saw you in bed with this *puta*," Corazón conceded.

"Don't you call me a whore just because I get pleasure in being with a man," Maribeth said. "I'll bet your bed isn't always empty."

Cord now had time to inspect the intruder. He admitted to himself that he had felt strangely excited for the few seconds their bodies were entangled. A strange reaction considering the circumstances. Like her brother Felipe, Corazón Lopez was darkly handsome. She wore no makeup except for a startling gash of red across her lips. Her figure, while not as lush as Maribeth's, was voluptuous, with curves made more tantalizing by the severely tailored *vaquero* outfit she wore. The black trousers, made for a man, seemed to accent her soft femininity. Her white silky blouse, still wet from the champagne, clung to her breasts.

"Who I sleep with is not your concern," Corazón told Maribeth. "And I don't care if you bed with a thousand men. But when gringos lie together, perhaps they conspire together to cheat me."

"You seem absolutely certain that you're not going to get a fair hearing," Cord said.

Corazón shrugged. "My people have always been cheated by the gringos."

"If you feel that way," Cord said, "why did you take a seat in a high-stakes poker game when the other players were all what you call gringos? Weren't you afraid of being cheated?"

Corazón looked at him thoughtfully, as if she was carefully considering her answer. "I came to the saloon that night to see Sam Buck about buying his freight line. He'd told Felipe he might be interested in selling. When I got there they'd already started playing and Sam told me he'd talk to me once the game was over. I like poker and I sat in to pass the time because I didn't know the betting would become so wild and foolish."

"She's lying, Cord," Maribeth broke in. "Why would Sam Buck want to sell his freight line? He's the richest man in town and he's buying everything in sight."

Corazón's dark eyes narrowed. "Do not call me a liar, *puta*. Sam Buck may be the richest man in town, but not the richest person."

"I assume you're claiming that honor?" Cord asked.

Corazón flushed proudly. "You may assume what you like."

"How much money did you lose that night?" Cord asked.

Corazón shrugged. "Just the price of an evening's diversion, until the last hand. That's when the betting became insane. I put in two thousand dollars before I dropped out." She shook her head. "Those men were betting their life's work."

"If you dropped out, how can you claim you were cheated?" Cord asked. "Seems to me you relinquished your claim to the pot."

They heard a clamor on the stairs, as if a herd of buffalo were racing toward the second floor.

"That will be Sebastian," Corazón said with grim satisfaction. "I believe he has Felipe with him. They will be very angry with you señor, I promise."

9.

"Where the hell did you hide my revolver?" Cord demanded, turning toward Maribeth.

"Last night I took your gunbelt off the bedpost and put it on the chair. It should be there under my petticoats."

Cord flung silky undergarments off the chair and hurriedly slid his Smith & Wesson Schofield .44 from the holster just as the two men noisily trampled across the door that Sebastian had knocked down earlier.

"Easy boys," Corazón cautioned as the men skidded to an abrupt halt. "Maybe I've let this thing go too far."

Felipe stared helplessly at Cord's gun while Sebastian just stood there dripping mud, looking like a dark waxen figure melting from exposure to the sun.

Cord held his revolver steadily on the two panting men. He pointed toward the window. "If the trip up here was too much effort, I can recommend the shortcut back down."

Felipe started toward Cord, but Corazón held up her hand.

"He has injured my friend and insulted you," Felipe told his sister. "I will not accept such treatment from any man."

"I provoked Sebastian to attack him," Corazón said. "And under the circumstances, he really wasn't rude to me."

Cord shook his head sadly. "I hope you're a good shot, Felipe, because any man who gets insulted as often and easily as you do needs a mastery of firearms to stay alive."

"Is that a challenge?"

"No, an observation. Now, I'd like the Lopez family, including faithful retainers, out of my room. Leave right now and you can pick your exit. In sixty seconds, you won't have a choice."

"Yes, I need some privacy," Maribeth whispered. The quilt around her body seemed to slip a little as Sebastian ogled her.

"Coming here this way was a mistake," Corazón admitted. Her eyes took in Cord, now clothed, but still barefooted. "Perhaps we can trust the gringo judge to listen to our side."

"Trust a gringo to listen to a Mexican?" Felipe looked at his sister as if she'd taken too much sun. "I'd sooner trust a rattler not to bite."

"You can be tiresome, Felipe," Corazón said as she led him and Sebastian out of the room.

Felipe stopped on the fallen door, teetering slightly as he delivered a threat. "This score will be settled, señor."

"God, look at the mess," Maribeth exclaimed,

staring at the muddied floor after they left. "That puddle is deep enough to have frogs in it."

Cord laughed. "Felipe's the manager here. He's the one responsible for getting this stuff cleaned up."

Maribeth leaned back on the crumpled bed, letting her quilt sink dangerously low. "Cord, darling, will you see about getting that door back up? The morning's still young."

"No time," Cord told her. "I hear more voices downstairs. It appears that a few people want to start the meeting early."

Standing at the head of the stairs, Cord saw two men below him conferring at a table far from the moldering corpse. The men bent forward, heads so close together their foreheads almost touched as they whispered inaudibly. An unlabeled bottle of whiskey, less than half full, sat between them as each man toyed with an empty shot glass. Corazón and Sebastian were nowhere in sight, but Felipe stood in his familiar place behind the bar, polishing glasses. The men hushed and glanced up as Cord descended the stairs.

One man rose and walked briskly to meet him at the foot of the stairs. He carried slightly too much weight on a frame that measured taller than Diamondback by half a head. Flab spilled over both ends of a wide belt buckle cinched too tight around his waist. His beefy face was lined with gullies and crevices, like raw land eroded by wind and water. A Stetson covered his head, but Cord could see gray mixed with brown hair in the man's bushy sideburns.

"Glad you could come, Diamondback," the man said, extending a callused hand. "I'm Jake Langely. Folks call me Longhorn." He waved the gnarled hand toward his table companion. "This here is Sam Buck."

The seated man waved two fingers toward Cord. "We treating you all right?" he asked. His voice floated toward Cord high and thin, completely without substance. "I told Felipe to give you first-class accommodations on the house."

"Felipe's giving me first-class treatment, all right," Cord said, bending his head toward the Mexican. Felipe waved a glass and bowed back.

Cord walked to the table and Sam Buck rose to offer Cord his hand. He was a short man, trim and dapper in a checkered suit that looked like it belonged on a whiskey drummer. A fringe of gray hair circled his ears below his bald scalp like a fallen halo. A pale complexion, pinkish white, suggested he spent all his time indoors. His cash-green eyes inspected Cord through the upper half of bifocals that rested against a small wart on his nose.

"We want this dispute settled fast," Langely told Cord. "This should be an easy one for you. The facts is clear as crystal."

"If everything's so obvious, why did you need me?" Cord asked.

Langely made a face, the crevices and gullies turning into small canyons. "You know how folks will fight over a dollar even when they got no rightful claim."

Cord didn't mind the idea of the two men trying to exercise influence before the others arrived. Hell, everyone else had, but he wanted to see how they felt about what they were doing. "I thought there was an agreement not to discuss the game until everyone could be present."

"That's right." Langely nodded. "We don't aim to tell you what happened, just how much is at stake here." He turned toward Felipe. "You can listen if you want to, Lopez. We ain't breaking the agreement."

Felipe shrugged. Cord thought he saw the Mexican mouth the word "gringos" under his breath.

"Just what do you have at stake?" Cord asked.

"Twenty-five years of my life," Langely said. Cord sensed a tone of desperation in the cattleman's voice. He also noticed that Sam Buck seemed very unsympathetic to Langely's predicament. "When Tim Brady put up his cattle ranch, I was forced to ante something of equal value to stay in the game. The only property I had to match the ranch was my herd of seven thousand Herefords. It's taken me the better part of a lifetime to accumulate that many cattle."

"You could have dropped," Cord reminded him. "Why did you bet so much?"

"I held the winning hand," Langely said. "I knew it then and I know it now. Why should I drop and let Brady bluff me out of the pot?"

"So you think the cards will show that you won Brady's ranch?"

"Damn right."

"Then why the urgency?" Cord asked. "What difference does another day or two make?"

Langely appeared uncomfortable. "I need Brady's land now. The mountain streams that water my property took a different turn this year. Brady's ponds are full and mine are dry holes. I gotta get that herd to water. Seems crazy to let 'em die when Brady's ranch will be mine the minute you turn up them cards.''

"Letting the winner take all isn't my only option," Cord reminded Langely. He noticed that Sam Buck kept silent, allowing Longhorn Langely to monopolize the conversation. "What did you bet?" Cord asked Buck. "Did you have the cash to match Brady's wager?"

"I put up title to the best freight line in the Southwest," Buck replied in his soft high voice. "It's worth more than Brady's ranch and Langely's cattle combined. The way this area's being settled, that freight line should be worth more than a million in a few years."

"If the line is so valuable, why did you offer to sell it to Corazón Lopez?"

Sam Buck's delicately colored skin reddened. "I can see how you come by your reputation. Sure didn't take you long to find out about that feeler I put out. But checking to see what the market will bring isn't the same thing as selling. I was just kidding Señorita Lopez along because I know she's hungry for the line. Had no intention of really selling."

"Are you sure you didn't put out the information to entice her over here that night?"

"Why would I do that?"

"Yeah, why would you? Maybe you needed another player for the card game."

Langely paced the floor of the General Lew Wallace, plainly out of patience with the conversation. "We don't need all these stupid questions from you, Diamondback. Just turn over the cards and pick the winner."

Deuce Devlin walked through the saloon's doors escorting Rosalyn Brady on his arm. He grinned, obviously having overheard Langely's last remark. "Making new friends as usual, Cord? The others are outside. It's time you heard the full story on that card game."

10.

Maribeth Adams came clattering down the stairs, applying makeup on the run. "Sorry I'm late," she said. "It's hard to get dressed when you don't have a damned door."

No one questioned her remark. The group sat around two tables close to the entrance of the General Lew Wallace, watching Cord with anticipation, sizing him up, judging the judge. Corazón, Rosalyn Brady, and Deuce Devlin sat at one table, Devlin eyeing Cord, his perpetual grin in place.

"These are the ground rules," Cord told the group after Maribeth settled in. "First I want to hear the story of that night from beginning to end. You all trusted Devlin to bring me here, so he gets to tell it. If anyone disagrees with his version, interrupt *politely* to correct the record. I'll interrupt from time to time to ask questions. Anyone who shouts or argues too loudly gets thrown out and forfeits the chance to tell his side. Any disagreement with the method?"

"Why go through with this farce?" Felipe asked

from his place behind the bar. "The only fair solution is to give each bettor his money back."

"Felipe's got a point, Cord," Devlin said. "The hand was never completed."

"Not by a damn shot," Langely interrupted. "Those players dropped out before Brady was shot. Any player who folds his cards loses his ante. They knew what they were risking. I say let the cards declare the winner. Why don't you put it to a vote?"

"Because if you could have settled by vote, you wouldn't have called for me," Cord said. "Now, before we get started, I want each of you to sit in the chair you occupied the night of the game. It'll help me picture what happened."

"Must we?" Maribeth complained. "The stink coming from that table is awful."

"Have you smelled your perfume?" Corazón asked Maribeth. "Or is that the smell you were referring to?"

"If I can stand it, no one else should have a problem," Rosalyn Brady said through clenched teeth. "Where do I sit, Mr. Diamondback? I wasn't even in town that night."

"Yes you were." Maribeth said. "I saw you at Sam Buck's general store."

"Maribeth's right," Sam Buck admitted. "Remember, you came in to look at frocks? Didn't buy anything, though. Said we didn't have anything up-to-date."

"I went back to my father's ranch long before the game got started," Rosalyn said angrily. "Felipe can vouch for me. He found me there when he rode out to tell me that father had been shot."

"Let's get down to the details of the game,"

Cord commanded. "We can discuss people's movements later."

The players sat down gingerly at the corpse's table, edging their chairs far from Brady, who still hadn't raked in that last pot.

"Is it my turn on stage?" Devlin asked with his easy grin. He lazily lit a cheroot, spending an eternity getting the tip glowing just right. "Maribeth served as our illustrious dealer," he started when he was satisfied with his smoke. "The original players were Sam Buck, Longhorn Langely, myself, and the late Mr. Brady, who still hasn't tired of the game. Corazón joined us about an hour later at Sam's invitation."

"First interruption," Cord said. "Sam, you set up the game, hired Maribeth, a professional dealer, and sent for Deuce Devlin, a known high-stakes player. Why? What prompted you to organize such a big game in a small town like Los Gordos?"

Sam carried one expression, a benign smile that spread across the width of his small pale face. "Los Gordos isn't big, but there are some big people living in it. Brady, myself, Longhorn, and Corazón, we're all considered successes. We wanted a little excitement without going all the way to Albuquerque to get it. Isn't that right, Longhorn?"

Langely looked at Buck in surprise. "That's not exactly true, Sam. Me and Tim wanted bigger stakes, sure, but neither of us expected the game we got. Course now I'm glad we had it because I'm holding the winning hand."

"Don't bet on it, Jake," Sam told him.

"I already did, my whole damn herd."

"My daddy wouldn't bet his ranch unless he was sure he had the best hand," Rosalyn said firmly.

"That's enough," Cord said. "Go on, Devlin."

"We started playing draw poker, table stakes," Devlin reported. "In Los Gordos that means any amount of money a player can throw on the table. The pots were decent, but nothing spectacular. Toward the end the betting was getting heavier as the players became impatient. As usual, I was winning, but there weren't any heavy losers, except Sam Buck." Devlin looked straight toward Buck and winked. "He's a lousy player and must have been out a few thousand."

"Nobody could win with the cards I was drawing," Sam complained. "I couldn't pick up a pair until that last hand."

"Tell me about that last deal," Cord asked.

"Sam was sitting in front of me, just like now," Maribeth cut in. Devlin raised an eyebrow at the interruption, but Cord motioned to let her continue. "Buck opened with a bet of five hundred. That was ten times the amount they'd been anteing for openers so I was shocked when everybody threw in money until Langely's turn. He was sitting anchor and raised Sam by five hundred. After that the betting got hot and heavy until each player had more than twenty-five hundred in the pot. Still nobody dropped. Then Sam Buck said he didn't have any more money but was convinced he held a winner. He offered to put up his freight line if anyone cared to match him."

"That's when I dropped out," Corazón said. "I wasn't going to gamble away my life's work over a game of cards."

"I couldn't cover that large a bet so I dropped too," Devlin said.

"What were you holding?" Cord asked Devlin. "You had already anted twenty-five hundred, so you must have had a damn good hand."

"My hole cards are my private business," Devlin said virtuously. "I don't show them to anyone unless he's paid the price."

"Okay, I suppose it's not important," Cord said. "What happened next?"

"Tim Brady said he'd match Sam's bet with the deed to his ranch," Maribeth went on. "Langely swallowed hard and put up a bill of sale on his herd of cattle. Sam looked like he would die when the two men covered his wager."

"Let me get this straight," Cord said. "This was just another high-stakes game until Sam Buck moved it into the atmosphere by betting his freight line. Is that right?"

"I was losing big and I had a cinch hand," Sam said. "I thought they'd fold and I'd get my money back."

"Did Brady do any of the raising?" Cord asked Maribeth.

"No, but he never hesitated calling."

"Brady sat in the middle between the two raisers, Sam Buck and Longhorn Langely," Cord observed. "That's the classical squeeze position."

Langely bristled. "I don't like what you're implying, Diamondback. I never cheated anyone in my life. I've known Brady for twenty years. The idea that Sam and I were in this together is ridiculous."

"What happened after all the bets were down?" Cord asked, ignoring Langely's tirade.

"I can't say for sure," Devlin replied. "I wasn't in the hand, so I went outside for a breath of air."

Cord shook his head in disbelief. "Devlin, you've been in some big games, but this was probably the biggest single pot you'd ever see. Are you telling me that a professional gambler like yourself would just walk away without waiting to see the outcome?"

Devlin's grin faded. "I couldn't stand to see all that money change hands, knowing that none of it was going over to my end of the table."

"I left too," Corazón said. "These men seemed to have gone mad. I couldn't stand to watch their madness, so I went home."

"I'd like a disinterested witness," Cord said. "Felipe, what did you see from behind the bar?"

"Unfortunately I was not at my station, señor," Felipe said. "I went outside to say good-bye to my sister. We had family business to discuss."

"So the only people left in the saloon were Langely, Sam Buck, Tim Brady, and you, Maribeth."

Maribeth smiled sweetly as she shook her head. "I was in the saloon, but I wasn't in the room. The men were all busy signing legal papers, so I had time to freshen up in the ladies' room. Dealing can be tiring work."

"They let you leave in the middle of a hand?" Cord asked, disbelieving.

"I know it's unusual, but signing over deeds takes time and I had been dealing for three hours without a break."

Cord sighed. "Everyone but the players sure rushed away from the card table. Okay, Sam, why don't you tell me what happened next?"

"The three of us cross-signed the legal documents. That took so long we all nailed our cards to the table to keep anyone from messing with our hands. Maribeth took forever and we waited for her to come back to finish dealing the hand. Tim Brady joked that he wasn't going to have much free time anymore because he'd be running a freight line plus another seven thousand head of cattle to look after. He laughed so hard he had a coughing fit. Then in the middle of a cough that sounded like he was trying to bring up phlegm, an explosion blasted out the back window and Brady slumped over the table."

Rosalyn Brady let out a soft cry.

"That's just the way it happened," Langely confirmed. "Some of Brady's blood splattered all over my shirt."

Cord walked to the rear window where the broken pane had been stuffed with rags to keep out the wind and rain. Shards of glass covered the floor, evidence that the fatal shot had come from outside the room.

"What was the weather like that night?" Cord asked.

Sam Buck wrinkled his brow. "The usual. Black clouds overhead with some rain. A typical night during our wet season."

Cord inspected the window. The unbroken panes were crusted with grime; no doubt it hadn't been washed since it was installed. He could barely see out the dirty panes, which meant that anyone outside would have similar difficulty seeing in. Yet on the night Brady was shot someone had stood outside in pitch blackness with rain pouring down on his face and blasted a hole in Brady's head from a distance of about thirty feet. A helluva shot under the circumstances. One thing for certain, the killer was a marksman.

"How long did it take Sheriff Richmond to get here after the shot was fired?"

Langely shrugged. "Everyone came running into the room at one time. "Corazón, Felipe, Maribeth. I guess Richmond came in with them."

"What did he do?"

"When we told Richmond what happened, he suggested making the poker hand state property. Nobody bought that, so we all agreed to keeping the cards nailed down until we could decide a winner. That's when Devlin suggested we send for you."

Cord looked over to Felipe. "After the shooting, Rosalyn Brady said you rode all the way to her father's ranch to tell her the news. Why? The Bradys aren't friends of yours."

Felipe glared toward Cord. "At a time of tragedy, one should forget old quarrels. Miss Brady had a right to know about her father."

"Felipe was brave to deliver such news," Rosalyn Brady said. "I know it wasn't an easy task for him and I'm grateful."

Devlin frowned. "Cord, I gotta remind you of what Felipe told you earlier. Quit poking around trying to discover Tim Brady's killer. You're here for one job and that's to pick the winner of the last poker hand."

"Doesn't anybody care who murdered my father?" Rosalyn Brady wailed.

An awkward silence filled the room. It was obvious that everyone's primary concern was the fortune represented by the poker pot.

"You've heard all the facts," Felipe said. "Now give each player his money back. Nothing else is fair."

"Let the cards decide," Langely boomed. "Those who dropped out have no further claim in this hand."

Cord sat down next to the dead man. "I've made several decisions. First, we bury Tim Brady. Keeping his corpse here serves no purpose."

"Thank you," Rosalyn Brady said.

"Next, I'm not declaring a misdeal. There's no evidence of improper procedure in the dealing of the cards or the betting. Brady's shooting shouldn't invalidate the results."

"The gringos only have justice for other gringos," Felipe said. Corazón nodded.

"That's the decision I wanted to hear, Diamondback." Langely actually rubbed the palms of his hands together. "Let's look at the hand so I can drive my cattle to my new ranch. Sam, I want to be generous about your freight line. You can buy it back at a fair price, or you got a week to vacate your office."

"Don't be so cocksure you have a winner," Sam replied. "I didn't bet with a pair of deuces."

"My daddy had the winner, I'm sure of it," Rosalyn said. Cord thought he heard more hope than certainty in her voice.

"Well, let's turn 'em over and see," Langely said impatiently.

"Not yet," Cord said.

"Why the hell not?" Langely's beefy face turned a darker shade of red. "I told you my cows need water."

"I still need one last piece of information," Cord told the cowman. "It'll take me two or three days to get it."

"Well, I'm turning mine over," Langely said defiantly. "I want you folks to see what a winner looks like."

"Display your hand if you like," Cord said. "There's no poker rule against it. But remember the game was draw poker. At the time Tim Brady was shot, nobody had yet discarded or called for new cards. That hand isn't over."

11.

Cord's Appaloosa splashed through the yard-wide brook the residents of Los Gordos sarcastically nicknamed the Rio Grande. The small stream, bone dry except during the rainy season, sealed off the town's Mexican section more effectively than an international boundary marker. Corazón's cantina, El Gato Negro, lay toward the far end of the still-muddy street, forcing Cord to endure a scattering of hostile stares as he trotted his horse down the crude thoroughfare.

Cord noticed that public improvements stopped where the Mexican district began. Gone were the wooden sidewalks, hitching posts, and water troughs that marked the Anglo part of town. The streets extended clear up to the doorsteps of the tiny adobe buildings. Cord saw movement behind the curtains, an occasional dark face peering at him. Where Sam Buck's name dominated the commercial enterprises "across the river," here, C. LOPEZ, PROPRIETOR seemed to be painted on every sign.

El Gato Negro stood out from neighboring buildings because it was the only two-story building

in the district. Cord gave the reins of his Appaloosa
to a small Mexican boy and walked through the
cantina's open door into a surprisingly bright room.
Early afternoon sunlight streamed through the door
and two latticed windows. Inside, whitewashed
adobe walls were spared of decoration except for
one outlandishly sized sombrero and a coiled
bullship. Wicker-covered clay jars filled with *pulque* sat on a blue tiled bar.

Cord cursed softly to himself when he spotted
Felipe earnestly talking to a customer in back of the
cantina. Sam Buck had specifically told him that
Felipe would be on duty at the General Lew
Wallace. Cord had hoped to speak with Corazón
without risking a confrontation with her brother.

"Hola, señor," Felipe said, his handsome face
splitting into a wide smile as he noticed Cord. "I
am delighted that you honor us, but don't you know
that this part of Los Gordos is dangerous for
gringos?"

"I'd like to speak with your sister," Cord said. "I
need some information about the game that didn't
come out during yesterday's meeting."

"Why should she tell you anything at all?"
Felipe asked. "Your judgment yesterday means that
she has lost all the money she wagered in that
cursed poker game."

"Maybe it's in her best interest," Cord said.
"She certainly can't lose any more by telling me
what I want to know."

"With gringos you can never be certain how
much you can lose," Felipe said. "Besides, Corazón is not here."

"When will she be back?"

"Quien sabe?" Felipe obviously enjoyed putting on his ignorant Mexican act. "The important thing is that you're here and I would not be a good host if I did not provide a reception you will long remember. Sebastian, look at who's come to call."

The room suddenly seemed darker. Cord turned and saw Sebastian's huge bulk standing in the doorway, blotting out the light. "I don't want a repeat of yesterday," Cord said. "I just want a chance to talk with Corazón."

"Did you hear that, Sebastian? The gringo judge wants no trouble. He injures you, steals my sister's money, and insults her, and now he wishes no trouble. Some things that are wished for are not possible, señor." Felipe motioned toward Sebastian, who advanced deliberately toward Cord. As he cleared the doorframe, the room became light and sunny again.

Cord pulled his Smith & Wesson, shaking his head. "Not again, fellas, I'm still tired from yesterday. This looks like another Mexican stand-off, if you'll pardon the expression."

Suddenly Cord's gun hand felt like a hot poker had been stroked across his fingers, burning them with a white-hot flame. Simultaneously, something cracked in his ear, as if a carbine had been fired in the room. Cord's gun clattered to the floor, discharging a round into the ceiling. Cord looked down at his gun hand and saw blood welling up in long slashes across his fingers that went clear to the bone. Pain gushed from his hand along with the blood. He turned toward Felipe and saw that the long bullwhip that had been used for wall decoration was now in the Mexican's hand.

"Did you say something about a Mexican stand-off?" Felipe asked with a satisfied smirk.

Sebastian plodded closer to Cord, now less than an arm's length away. Cord feinted his useless right hand and threw a left hook into the giant's midsection, burying his fist into his stomach. Air rushed out of Sebastian's mouth like a punctured balloon as he doubled over. Cord kneed him in the face and watched with satisfaction as the giant slowly crumpled.

"You do not fight fairly, señor," Felipe said, pulling his whip hand back for another crack at Cord.

"Maybe you could give me a lesson in fairness by dropping that whip and calling off Sebastian."

Felipe shrugged and sent the long black leather snaking toward Cord's face. The tip cracked less than an inch away from his eye. Cord grabbed a wooden cantina stool and held it in front of him for protection, but the whip lashed again, splitting the wood into kindling. Cord's left hand now held only a single stool leg, which he hurled toward Felipe's head, causing him to duck.

Cord used the few seconds to scan the floor for his revolver. Where the hell had it fallen? There! Next to the bar! Cord dived for the gun, but Felipe's whip cracked again, sending the revolver sliding to the far corner of the room.

Sebastian rose slowly and lumbered toward Cord with a look of intense determination on his huge face. Cord pulled one of the clay *pulque* jars off the bar and smashed it into Sebastian's skull, sending earthen shards and *pulque* spraying across the floor. Felipe's whip lashed across Cord's back, biting through his shirt and slicing into his skin. A tidal wave of pain swept over him. All he could think of was that the whiplash wouldn't show because his back was already a mass of scars. No one would be able to tell there had been an addition.

Sebastian got up again, staggering as he lunged toward Cord. The stink of *pulque* completed his drunken image. Cord felt he could have put him down again, but right now he wanted the giant between him and Felipe's whip. He allowed the giant to close in, and Sebastian raised his long arms as if he planned to embrace Cord. Cord darted sideways to avoid the hug, but his foot skidded on the wet floor, allowing Sebastian to enfold him in his tree-branch arms. The air rushed out of Cord's chest as if he were a concertina playing a wild song. He held his body limp, offering no resistance, but he felt he was in a wine press, his vital juices being squeezed out of him.

"That's it, amigo." Felipe chortled: "I knew that once this gringo was in your grasp he could not escape. Show him the strength of our people."

Cord tried smearing his bloody right hand into Sebastian's eyes, but he couldn't get the leverage. Sebastian's face contorted as he increased the pressure. Cord's strength drained out of him; Sebastian's face faded out of focus. He raised his foot high—even that took more effort than he thought he could muster—and smashed his heel down hard on the giant's instep. He felt his bootheel cutting through the brittle foot bones in Sebastian's arch as the giant opened his mouth in a silent scream. He crumpled to the floor, turning his face toward Felipe in a silent plea for help.

"What have you done?" Felipe screamed. "You've crippled my friend." His whip hand pulled back for another attack on Cord. "This time I go for the face. Have you ever seen a man whose eyes have been shattered by a whip? The pupils actually burst and mix with the whites, looking like bits of glass in a milky sea."

Cord kept darting and feinting, changing direction to make Felipe's target more difficult to hit. The cantina floor was slippery with *pulque* and Cord's own blood, which still flowed from his whipped right hand. Felipe's whip hissed through the air and bit into Cord's shoulder, tearing off a small hunk of flesh. The shock sent him spinning, and he landed on his back on the wet floor. Cord scrambled on his knees for the protection of the bar's underlip, knowing that Felipe couldn't reach him there unless he came out to the customer side. Felipe cursed. Cord could hear his footsteps as he stomped around to the other side. Cord reached his good hand up to the top of the bar and pulled down another jar of *pulque*. As Felipe turned the corner, Cord slid the jar across the floor toward the Mexican's feet. The jar tumbled him over like a ninepin. Cord pulled himself erect, rushed toward Felipe, and chopped him in the base of the neck as he tried to rise. The Mexican's eyes rolled forward in his head as he fell backward on top of Sebastian.

Cord retrieved his Smith & Wesson, crawling because he was unable to stand erect. He bandaged his right hand with cloth torn from Sebastian's shirt. He'd only received three whiplashes, but his loss of blood was serious. Nothing stayed in focus. He thought he saw a figure standing over him. Who was it? Sebastian or Felipe?

"What have you done to my cantina?" Cord heard a voice say from a very long distance. "My brother, my servant, what have you done to them? You'll pay for this, Cord Diamondback." Cord opened his mouth to say he had already paid, but black shades moved across his eyes as he slumped over unconscious.

12.

"Don't expect this patch-up to last. I'm no nurse and those cuts on your fingers go clear to the bone." The voice Cord heard, but couldn't see, was deep and throaty and feminine. The woman spoke with a quiet authority, as if giving orders came naturally to her.

Cord's eyelids fluttered open. He tried to focus his vision on the blurred face behind the voice. He felt light-headed and giddy, almost as if he'd drunk too much wine. The feeling was vaguely pleasant except for the persistent pain in his right hand. He concentrated on the pain, using it to battle back to full consciousness. He took a slow, deep breath, filling his lungs with the heady fragrance of an exotic flower. Not the time to be concerned about a scent, but what was it? Jasmine probably. His eyes cleared and he saw Corazón Lopez bending over him, her olive skin turned to dark ivory by the day's waning light drifting through the room's single window.

"How long have I been unconscious?"

Corazón frowned, busy tending his wounds.

"Too long. I would have sent for the doctor, but he won't make house calls in the Mexican district."

Feeling started coming back in all of Cord's limbs. With the feeling came pain, sharp and raw. He felt his skin had been scraped by a fish scaler. "I see we're on the second floor. Surely you didn't drag me up here by yourself?"

Corazón's mouth turned upward. "I forced my brother, Felipe, to carry you to my room before he went back to work at Sam Buck's saloon."

"You must be very persuasive. The last time I saw Felipe, he didn't seem inclined to do me favors."

"We had a difficult time because he wasn't in much better shape then you are." Corazón bent closer and rolled Cord's shirt up past his powerful chest. A scarlet welt, long and wide as a garter snake, stood out against his stomach muscles. "Felipe's whip," Corazón whispered as she reached for a clay jar. She dipped her hand in the jar and generously lathered salve across the welt. Cord felt the salve cooling and soothing the lash mark. Corazón bent her body so close to his face that the scent of her tropical perfume masked the pungent odor of the medicine.

"Can you sit up and take off your shirt?" she asked, putting down the jar. "I want to take a look at your shoulder wound."

"The shoulder's fine." Cord quickly rolled his shirt down past his waist. He felt lucky that Corazón hadn't removed it while he lay unconscious. The mass of scars on his back, jumbled one on top of the other like a miniature logjam, would have revealed his identity. What would she do if she knew the true identity of Cord Diamondback?

Corazón screwed her face in disgust at Cord's refusal of help. "It seems Felipe doesn't have the Los Gordos monopoly on machismo. Let your shoulder fall off for all I care. In fact, hombre, if you're feeling so much better, why don't you just walk out of here now?"

Cord nodded. "That might be a good idea. I appreciate what you've done for me, Señorita Lopez, but it's time to go." His right hand was encased in a blood-soaked bandage. He used his left to brace his body as he tried to rise. He half rose and the arm propping him up started to waver and bend like a sapling in a high wind. The giddy feeling in his head turned to dizziness as he fell back on the bed. "Maybe I'll rest here for just a few minutes longer."

Corazón giggled, an uncharacteristically girlish laugh that Cord found charming despite his predicament. "Ah, you've kindly decided to take advantage of my hospitality, though I don't know why I offer it. Did you know that you crippled poor Sebastian? He won't be able to walk on that smashed foot for the better part of a year."

Cord shrugged, unconcerned. "Perhaps the people to blame for his injury are those who used him to fight his battles."

"Meaning me and Felipe?"

"You both unleashed him at me the way you would a fighting dog. When the dog gets kicked, the master's to blame."

Corazón's dark handsome face turned serious.

"Yes, you're right. Sebastian's been with our family so long we treat him like a possession."

"If you resent what I've done to your servant, why have you brought me up here?"

She looked at him oddly, as if wondering about the reason herself. "You were unconscious and bleeding badly. If I had left you where you were, without treatment, you might have bled to death. I don't wish anyone's death, and Felipe would have been charged with murder."

Cord grinned. "I'll bet you used that argument on your brother when you persuaded him to help bring me up here."

She laughed with him, a strong laugh this time, which showed even white teeth inside a generous mouth. "You seem to know the Lopez family very well for such a short acquaintance."

"A short, painful acquaintance," he reminded her.

Corazón sat on the bed, her hip almost touching him. She dipped a damp cloth in a bowl mixed with oil and cinnamon and carefully wiped dried blood from his head and body. The cloth cooled his skin, easing the pain and leaving a light, spicy odor.

Cord felt drowsy again, lulled by the darkness of the room, her light touch on his body, and the delicate aroma now pervading the room. Still, he had come here for information. "Why are you so concerned about the twenty-five hundred dollars you lost in the poker game? I know that isn't a small sum, but you obviously can afford it."

"Because the game wasn't honest," Corazón said. "I was cheated out of my money. I have no proof, but I *know* it."

"That doesn't explain your behavior. I'd expect anything of Felipe, but you came storming into my room with Sebastian, prepared to do great bodily harm. Over twenty-five hundred dollars?"

She thought about his question, then nodded. "The people on this side of town, my people, look up to the Lopez family. Felipe is educated and I am a business success. We are proof that a Mexican can do anything a gringo can do. But if we allow the gringos to cheat us, then it shows that we are not truly equal."

Cord sighed. "Don't you ever get tired of being a symbol?"

Corazón looked at him appreciatively. "The judge shows some understanding. Sometimes it is very tiring . . . and lonely."

"Lonely?"

"Many of the Mexican men in Los Gordos resent my success. A woman's place is at the hearth, patting tortillas and all that nonsense. The others are intimidated by my wealth and afraid to approach too closely. Except for my brother, I enjoy very little masculine companionship."

"Your prejudice is showing, Corazón. Why not keep company with a gringo?"

She shrugged and continued to wash his body. Her silky blouse was not cut low, but as her body leaned over him, he could see the beginning of the cleft between her large, firm breasts. The cleft seemed a passageway to a dark valley, warm, mysterious, and inviting. Her hand moved under his shirt, spreading a thin layer of scented oil on his chest. Despite his weakness, he felt the soft, insistent motion around his nipples sexually exciting. Corazón noticed the new look that came to his eye, blushed, and quickly removed her hand.

"Perhaps you have recovered well enough to leave after all." She started to rise, but Cord grabbed her hand in a weak grasp that wouldn't have contained a hummingbird. She sat back down, making no protest, then gently laid her hand on his chest, his hand on top of hers.

Cord reached behind her neck and pulled her head closer to him. She sighed softly as her face bent down, her long hair caressing his cheeks, the jasmine smell almost overpowering. She kissed him gently, covering his lips with hers, and brought her fingers along the side of his face. Cord's tongue probed, insistent, but Corazón kept her lips tightly closed, resisting the pressure. Suddenly she gave a soft moan and opened her mouth wide, as a conquered city opens its gates to the invading enemy. His tongue entered the portal, seeking hers, but she teased and evaded him, darting away into the far corners of her mouth as if this were a new variation on the game of hide and seek.

Cord's hand moved to her waist, pulling her closer as she leaned her body against his wounded shoulder.

"Ouch!" Cord yelled.

Corazón broke away, the spell broken, and rose quickly. "We can't do this. You're—"

"Don't worry about my injuries. This is the best treatment I can imagine."

"No, I don't mean that. I can't make love to a gringo."

Cord slumped back in his bed. "I'm disappointed in you."

Corazón walked toward the window, looking out as the day's last light moved beyond the horizon. It was that short, magic time between twilight and nightfall when shape and dimension seem to change. She stayed near the window for a time, watching night fall, before pulling down the shade, making the room completely dark, and turning back to Cord. "Sometimes I disappoint myself."

He heard the rustle of clothing falling to the floor but saw only the dim outline of her curved body in the dark. He felt cold for an instant as the thin blanket was lifted from the bed, then the shift of the mattress from the weight of her body. He reached for her as she slipped into bed.

"Tenderly, tenderly," she murmured, moving her naked body against his. She felt soft and incredibly warm, her nipples pressed against his radiating heat like lit lanterns. Cord found her mouth in the darkness. She opened it wide, plunging her tongue between his lips, finding his tongue, playfully flicking the tip, and finally sucking it into her own mouth and holding it a gentle captive between her satiny lips.

Cord felt frustrated because he had only one unbandaged hand with which to explore her lush body. He cupped her breast with his good left hand, feeling the firm mound topped by a nipple that seemed as big and hard as an unshelled pecan. His fingers toyed with the nipple until she moaned and draped one leg over his, her silky thigh brushing up against his rock-hard penis. His own thigh felt the warm wetness between her legs as she pressed closer to him.

Corazón broke off their kiss and moved her body

up the bed, raising it slightly until her breast dangled over Cord's face. She slowly traced the nipple against his eyes, nose, forehead, and finally his mouth. He kissed the velvety softness, rimming the nipple with his tongue, sucking it into his mouth until it glistened with his saliva.

"Oh, yes," Corazón hissed softly, pressing her body down until her breast was crushed against his face, almost smothering him.

She spread her legs wider, imprisoning his thigh between them. Her hips moved gently against his thigh in a circular motion. Cord's good hand found the curve of her buttocks, stroking and seeking and straying ever downward until the hand approached her vagina from the rear. Her thick pubic hair felt damp and soft. Cord thrust his middle finger between her vagina lips, the palm of his hand still pressed against her buttocks. He felt her vagina shudder as his finger plunged into the mossy depths.

Corazón's hand traced down the length of his stomach until she reached his penis. "That's mine," she said, grasping the base so tightly that he almost cried out. Her hand traveled up his shaft, pulling his skin along with it. Her fingers massaged his tip until a few drops of semen spilled from the crack. She spread them like a lip balm on her mouth and kissed him again, giving him a salty, musky taste of himself.

Cord thrust a second finger into her vagina and Corazón bucked her hips toward his hand in a series of short movements. His two fingers were now buried in her vagina past the first knuckle. The thrust of her body against his probing fingers came shorter and quicker. Her body thrashed against his as little mewling sounds, almost like an animal crying, came from her mouth. She spasmed, losing complete control, her vagina nibbling at his fingers like a school of fish taking bait.

"We Mexicans are passionate," she said, smiling and holding Cord's still-hard penis in her hand. "Beware, once you get us aroused."

"Don't speak in the plural," Cord said. "One Mexican woman is all I can handle."

"But we still have to take care of this," she said, milking Cord's penis until he felt pressure building in his loins.

Corazón straddled his lower stomach, the trunk of her body bent over so her breasts brushed against his chest. She slid her body downward, still holding his penis and guiding it into her thoroughly wet vagina. It was tight and warm, and Cord grunted as he worked his penis deeper inside her until their pubic hair mingled and matted together.

One silky thigh caressed each of his sides as she slowly rocked over him. She placed her arms around the back of his neck, pressing her breasts against his chest, their nipples fighting a separate war. She buried her face into his neck, sending her tongue exploring upward until it found the inside of his ear. He pulled her face around, his lips seeking her open mouth. Their bodies moved faster, groin grinding against groin. His tongue plunged into her mouth in unison to his penis stabbing into her vagina.

The mewling sounds were coming from Corazón's throat again. Cord could feel her vagina constricting in pulsating waves that started his testicles boiling. He released the pressure, slamming his penis into her as his semen rushed up his shaft and out the tip. He spurted a gusher. Corazón sat bolt upright, burying his spurting penis even deeper inside her. Her body twisted and rocked wildly as he drained himself dry.

"I should have met you much earlier in my life," she said, toying with his testicles as they snuggled together. "Is that why you came here today? So I would learn to appreciate gringos?"

"I'm not here to teach you tolerance." Cord laughed. "I wanted to ask you about Sam Buck. Do you think he was seriously looking for a buyer for his freight line?"

"That's what he told Felipe. I believed it enough to visit him that evening. Some of Sam's businesses haven't been doing too well."

"How do you know that? And you'd better stop doing what you're doing, or there'll be a new international incident."

She giggled. "You no like de action south of de border?" she asked, affecting a heavy Mexican accent. "It's hard to keep financial secrets in a small town like Los Gordos. Sam's credit was bad down at the bank."

"Were you prepared to make him an offer? What would have been a fair price for the line?"

"I don't know; I'd have to see Sam's books. Oh, isn't this fascinating!" she exclaimed as Cord's penis began to show an interest in her handiwork. "Looks like we could have another shoot-out."

"Was the freight line worth Tim Brady's ranch?" Cord found he was beginning to lose interest in her answers as his attention was diverted to her busy hand.

"Probably more," Corazón said. "It's the only freight line serving Albuquerque and Santa Fe. Now shut up and get over here. We don't have much time together before you leave town."

He looked at her, puzzled. "What gives you the idea that I'm leaving town?"

She rose on one elbow. "I don't know anything about your background, Diamondback, but I suspect you'll be riding out soon. Kane Richmond's back in town. He must have ridden all night from Fort Sumner to get here. He sure looked pleased when he learned you were still in Los Gordos. Richmond said that was the best financial news he'd ever heard."

13.

"You're smooth as glass, Diamondback, I'll give you that." Kane Richmond's bloodless lips creased, but no one would mistake the look of his cadaverous face for a smile. "No one in Los Gordos dares bother me when I'm taking target practice, yet here you are asking if we have any business. I'd have bet wages you'd be hightailing for Mexico by now."

Richmond had a dozen assorted beer and whiskey bottles dangling by their necks from the low limb of an elm tree. Spent cartridges lay at his feet like seeds waiting to sprout.

"Why should I run, Sheriff?" Cord tied up his Appaloosa out of the line of fire. His bandaged hand dangled uselessly next to his holstered Smith & Wesson. He saw no point in waiting for Richmond to come to him. If the man had evidence connecting him to Christopher Deacon, Cord wanted to know now.

"You'd know better than anyone why you should skedaddle," Richmond said.

Cord looked puzzled. "I'm sure you didn't find any posters on Cord Diamondback."

Richmond loaded live cartridges into his Colt .45. "That's a lawyer's answer," he said, sighting down the barrel. "You have any training in that area?"

"A judge should have a legal background."

Richmond moved over to the tree and set the bottles swaying. He retraced his steps back to his original spot and stood motionless. His hand whipped to his holster with a blur that Cord couldn't follow. The Colt kicked in his hand and six bottles shattered, sending a shower of glass to the ground beneath the elm tree. The sheriff glanced back at Cord to see if he appreciated the feat.

"That's one way to get rid of your empties," Cord said.

Richmond reloaded, eyeing Cord carefully. "Old Sheriff Saunders in Fort Sumner never throws anything away. He's got a back room filled with posters that go back ten or twelve years. After a few hours digging, I came up with an old poster on a man who could be your twin brother. Only he went by a different handle: Christopher Deacon. That name mean anything to you?"

"Of course it does. Everyone's heard of the man who killed Senator Fallows." He really knows, Cord thought. Or does he? He'd better hear the sheriff out, see how much he knew and how much he guessed. Cord had seen the wanted posters when they first were plastered over every town in the Southwest. A positive identification based on those sketches would be very difficult.

Richmond waved toward the bottles. "Care to try your luck?" He appeared to notice Cord's bandages for the first time. "Hurt your gun hand?" Unexpectedly, he reached over and squeezed Cord's hand hard.

"Hey, that hurts like hell!"

"Sorry," Richmond said. The apology did not register on his face. "I've known a man to wrap a derringer in bandages like those."

Cord tried to look insulted at Richmond's insinuation. Actually, the two-shot derringer he'd borrowed from Deuce Devlin earlier in the day was tightly strapped under his right armpit.

The sheriff motioned at the bottles again. "Care to try with your left hand?"

Cord shook his head. "I couldn't hit Pike's Peak with my off hand." No point in telling Richmond that he practiced an hour every day and was equally adept with either hand. But he knew he wasn't as fast as Richmond. Maybe no one was.

Richmond snorted contemptuously and snaked the Colt out of his left holster. His pistol roared, the shots so close together they sounded like they came out of a Gatling gun. The necks of the already-shattered bottles burst, leaving empty strings dangling from the tree branch.

Richmond looked back at Cord proudly, waiting for praise. Cord stood silent. "This fella, Deacon, the one you're a ringer for." There was an annoyed tone in the sheriff's voice. "I checked and the rewards are still outstanding. More than ten thousand dollars in all."

"Let's quit the cat and mouse, Richmond. You've decided I'm Deacon on the basis of a faded picture on an old poster. You're setting yourself up to look like a fool."

Richmond shrugged. "If I'm right, I'm a fool with ten grand in my pocket."

"Don't spend the money just yet."

"That's good gunslinger talk, Diamondback. You got just the right amount of threat into your small speech." Richmond's eyes strayed to Cord's bandaged hand. "But style ain't enough against a professional like me. I'd give you an education, but that bad hand of yours wouldn't look good for me at the inquiry."

Cord waited for the moment when he could pull the derringer. No point in waiting any longer. Richmond knew his true identity.

"Yessir," the sheriff continued. "I could maybe collect a reward on you, but then I'd lose out on a chance for a lot more."

Cord stopped thinking about drawing his gun. Richmond had something in mind. That's why the conversation had gone on so long.

The sheriff's hollow face grew pensive. "You think I'm fast, Diamondback?"

"You fishing for compliments, Sheriff? I saw you shoot today."

Richmond looked at his hands, flexing his fingers like a concert pianist ready to begin a long piece. "I can pump two shots into the belly of a nonprofessional before his gunsight clears leather. But believe it or not, I used to be faster." His eyes stared off somewhere, focusing on the glory days of the past. "Five years from now, who knows? Some raw cowhand who only practices an hour a day might take me."

Cord smiled to himself. He practiced an hour a day.

Richmond sighed. "I built my reputation going up against men who'd lost their edge. I don't suppose things have changed much. Someday the punks will come looking for me."

"I can't believe you're asking for my sympathy, Sheriff," Cord said.

Richmond whirled suddenly, his Colt smashing the remaining hanging bottles into small pieces, then reducing the pieces until the area under the elm tree danced and sparkled as the sun reflected on the broken glass.

"I can protect you, Diamondback," Richmond said when he finished the barrage.

"From what? The only threats I've had have come from you."

Richmond almost managed a smile. "That's part of it. I think I can earn ten thousand dollars for bringing you in, but that's peanuts compared to the fortune in this town waiting for somebody to pick it up. I mean it's lying there on the table."

Cord laughed out loud. "You mean the poker hand? Most of that pot is in property."

"So what? The ownership papers are all signed over. I figure the ranch, cattle, and freight line would bring at least three hundred thousand in a quick cash-out. Now, what if the town of Los Gordos confiscates the pot? I could invent some legal reason to fine the players and sell the property to satisfy the fines."

"It wouldn't work. Nobody would buy the property from you because you couldn't offer clear title."

"That's why you have a chance to ride away

from here with me forgetting what I learned in Fort Sumner. The players have all signed a paper agreeing to abide by any decisions you make. If you decide my fine is justified, that's all the legal excuse I need. The property gets turned over to me and I find a buyer at distress prices."

"There's no basis for that kind of decision," Cord protested. "Making bad decisions like that would ruin my reputation."

"No decision that saves your life is a bad one," Richmond said. "Tell you what, you can keep the cash that was in the pot. That's not a bad deal, Diamondback. You get more than ten thousand bucks and your freedom."

Cord shook his head. "I can't see Sam Buck and Longhorn Langely standing still for that kind of blatant swindle. You'd have a dozen lawsuits on your hands, tying up the property."

"Who said they'd be standing at all? They could get shot just the way Brady did. The property would be sold before their heirs knew what was going on."

Cord shook his head. "Richmond, you have more imagination than I gave you credit for. You set up this deal starting with the killing of Tim Brady."

Richmond blinked at Cord in surprise. "Who said I killed Brady? I was in the General Lew Wallace when it happened."

"Witnesses said you rushed into the saloon seconds after the shot was fired."

"Who the hell says that?" Richmond shouted. "I make my pukey living in this town taking a cut out of the gambling. I had just walked over to get my share. I arrived in the saloon seconds *before* the shot was fired."

Cord wondered if Richmond was lying. Not one of the witnesses had placed him in the saloon until after the shooting. Yet why would the sheriff openly talk of killing Buck and Langely and deny shooting Brady? Maybe because the one murder was already accomplished. Admitting it would give Cord a hold on him. Just talking about shooting someone wasn't a crime until after it happened.

"What about Rosalyn Brady?" Cord asked. "She stands to inherit her father's ranch. You planning on killing her too?"

Richmond screwed up his face. "Plugging a woman in these parts tends to rile people."

"You talking from experience, Sheriff?"

"That an insult? I never plugged no white woman. If you can keep her out of the way until this is over, she might come out of this okay."

"You mean standing, but without her father's ranch?"

"Look at it this way. The odds are two to one her old man held a losing hand. We're probably not cheating her out of anything."

"You keep saying 'we,' Richmond. I haven't agreed to anything."

"You don't have any choice. Cooperate with me, or I turn you in. I'd be disappointed, but I'd still collect ten thousand bucks. And who knows? Without you around, I still might be able to pull the deal off."

"I'm not Deacon," Cord repeated. "So you wouldn't collect a cent on me. Besides, I never said

I wouldn't do it, I only stated that I didn't like your proposition."

"I suppose you have a better one?"

"I sure do," Cord said. "I want half of everything sitting on that poker table."

14.

Cord wiped his brow with his bandanna. Sweat formed tiny rivulets and streamed down his neck and back, soaking his shirt. He lowered his Stetson against the powerful noonday sun and let the Appaloosa move at its own pace. He was in no hurry to reach Tim Brady's ranch. The horse waded through one of the many small ponds that Longhorn Langely coveted. Cord was no cattleman, but he could see Brady had a rich spread with plenty of water and rich grass. Well worth stealing, he thought.

He crested one hill and caught sight of a square pink object lying at the edge of one of the ponds. He moved down the hill toward it until he recognized the object as a blanket. A light-colored Morgan, still saddled, was tied to a sapling near the blanket, but Cord couldn't spot the horse's owner. He had almost reached the shore when he noticed a series of ripples toward the far edge of the pond. A dark round object, about the size of a duck, floated in the center of the ripples, like a bull's-eye in a watery target.

Cord was pushing the Appaloosa into the water when he heard a female voice cry out, "Go away, I'm swimming here." He peered across the pond and saw that the floating object was a head encased in a ruffled bathing cap. Rosalyn Brady.

"Will you go away, please?" she repeated. "I'd like some privacy."

"I've got to talk to you, Miss Brady," Cord shouted down to her as he backed his horse out of the pond. "I'll turn my back if you're not wearing any clothes."

"Of course I'm wearing my bathing costume," Rosalyn Brady retorted. "Do you think I've adopted the primitive customs of the frontier?" She emerged from the water, clad in a striped wool bathing suit that descended to her knees. The suit had a billowy overskirt sewn with the same ridiculous ruffles as her bathing cap. Water streamed from the ruffles down her shapely calves as she waded petulantly toward the shore. Cord thought the costume must be the latest fashion from the East, or maybe even Paris. The wet wool clung to every curve of her slender, just-ripened body, making the young woman look absolutely ravishing.

"It's so hot out here," she complained. "And so dull. I decided to take a dip to cool and amuse myself." She removed her bathing cap, letting her long tawny hair tumble free to her shoulders. "I suppose I must speak with you, though, seeing as your decision will shape the rest of my life." She looked at Cord from the corner of her eye. "How does it feel to wield so much power?"

"I know the money is important to you," he said, "but it shouldn't shape the rest of your young life. Even if you lose the ranch, you can still return to Europe and marry your fiancé."

Rosalyn Brady's pretty face pouted. "You think he'd still marry me if I were impoverished? That's not the way the aristocracy does things."

"You know he's marrying you for your money and you don't care? That seems more primitive than any custom we have here in the West."

Rosalyn picked up a towel and patted her face dry. "I'll be a countess," she said defensively. "Alfred's genteel, cultured, educated: everything that people in the American West are not. He's descended from the Bourbon kings, though I don't expect that to mean much to you."

"Which branch?" Cord asked. "French or Spanish."

Rosalyn looked at him curiously. "French."

"Then there's not much chance of his ever sitting on a throne."

She now stared at him openly. "How do you happen to know so much about European royalty?"

"I'm interested in history, among other things."

"You don't reveal all of yourself, do you, Cord Diamondback?" Rosalyn rewarded him with a warm smile. "Some knowledge of the French language and European history, obviously educated, legal ability, what other facets have you kept hidden?"

"I'm more interested in what you've kept hidden."

Her smile dissolved. "What do you mean?"

"I want the real reason you were in town the afternoon your father was killed. I don't believe you went shopping for frocks at Sam Buck's general store. Not with your taste for fashion."

Rosalyn Brady's fair, creamy complexion turned a rosy pink. "I went to visit Mr. Buck to get an independent appraisal of the value of my father's ranch. Alfred's family wanted to know how much I'd be bringing into the marriage."

"Why didn't you ask your father?"

"The appraisal had to come from an outside source. Besides, my father would get furious whenever I talked of marrying Alfred."

Cord considered what the young woman had told him. "Would your father have disinherited you after the marriage?"

Her face took on an alarmed look. "No, of course not. My father loved me. He didn't like the idea of me living in Europe permanently, but he never would have taken me out of his will. It's cruel of you to suggest something like that."

"What value did Sam Buck place on the ranch?"

"He said for the right buyer the ranch would bring at least two hundred and fifty thousand dollars because of the water."

"Why do you think your father would risk all that in a poker game?"

Her face lighted. "That what I told you earlier. My father wasn't a plunger. He wouldn't bet everything he worked his life for unless he felt absolutely certain he would win. He must have held a hand that couldn't be beaten."

"That would be a royal flush," Cord told her.

"A what?"

"A hand that couldn't be beaten. That's a royal flush. In poker there's nothing better."

"Then that's what he had," Rosalyn declared. "A royal flush. I'm sure of it. My father was killed because he held the winning hand."

Cord shook his head. "But he obviously wasn't killed by another player at the table. The shot definitely came from outside the room."

"A confederate could have done it," Rosalyn said. "I don't trust that awful Langely. He's really after my father's ranch."

"It's possible," Cord admitted. "There was time to arrange something when Maribeth left the room. But why? The killer isn't necessarily going to win the pot."

"How would I know?" Rosalyn Brady cried. "I just know that everything in that pot belongs to me. Alfred will be pleased when he learns the size of my dowry." She replaced her silly bathing cap. "Now I'd like to go back in the water."

Cord turned to leave. "Be at the General Lew Wallace tomorrow afternoon. I'm deciding the poker-hand winner then."

She looked back at him thoughtfully. "It's awfully hot and you're perspiring, Mr. Diamondback."

"The sun usually has that effect," he said, heading for his horse.

Rosalyn waded out until the water reached midthigh, then called to Cord. "Swimming alone isn't much fun. Will you join me?"

"Mixed bathing?" he said, pretending to be scandalized. "What would your friends on the Continent say?"

"We're cosmopolitans, not Puritans," she replied, splashing water toward Cord and diving under the waves.

Cord shed his boots and denim pants, looking out across the pond for Rosalyn. She seemed to have disappeared.

The water felt tepid and brackish, but the firm, sandy bottom allowed him to wade out to his chest. He scanned the pond's surface for Rosalyn when the girl suddenly burst from the depths like a projectile and thoroughly soaked him.

"Prudish, prudish," she chanted, pointing at his shirt as she swam around him in a terribly inefficient dog paddle. "Don't you know that it's quite acceptable for a gentleman to be bare-chested when swimming, even though ladies may be present?"

Cord wondered about her sudden change in mood. She'd first demanded complete privacy but now acted like a coquette. Whatever the reason, he found her high spirits a delightful change from the pretentious young woman who had bailed him out of Kane Richmond's jail. "We're not well enough acquainted for that intimacy."

She reddened at the word "intimacy," then swept her open hand across the surface of the water, sending a miniature tidal wave surging toward Cord. "I'll bet you took your shirt off for Maribeth Adams the other night."

"You'd lose that bet." Cord laughed. No point in telling her he never took off his shirt for anyone.

Rosalyn suddenly dipped beneath the surface. Cord peered into the depths of the murky pond but could see nothing. He felt something surround his legs and tug hard, pulling him off balance and submerging his head beneath the waves. When he managed to break back to the surface, spitting out pond water, Rosalyn floated a few feet away, shrieking with laughter.

He inhaled deeply, dived under the water and searched until he spotted her legs looking like slender columns growing from the pond's bottom. He kicked toward her and placed a hand behind each of her thighs, pedaling forward until his shoulders gently bumped her pelvis, then heaved upward, sending her body hurtling out of the water. She did a half somersault in the air and landed on her back with a flop that sprayed water fifteen feet. Rosalyn backstroked, shrieking and making a tremendous splash with her legs as he pursued her.

Cord dived under again, emerging to catch her by her slender waist. She screamed and laughed as she twisted out of his grasp, apparently not carrying that her struggles occasionally caused his hands to wander across her firm breasts. He felt her nipples harden beneath the wet wool suit. Her breath came faster and harder as her giggling stopped.

"I think we've had enough water sports," Cord said, dropping his hands from her waist.

"No, you don't," she said, like a child unwilling to give up a game. She dipped beneath the water and encircled his hips with her arms, trying to yank him under. As she tugged, her arms brushed against his penis and he felt it stretch and stiffen despite himself.

"That's enough," Cord said, reaching down and pulling her head out of the water.

In reply she squirted his face with a mouthful of water. He grabbed her around the waist to give her a dunking. Her wet, slender body, plastered against his, wriggled and squirmed as he tried to tilt her backward into the pond. She threw her arms around his neck to keep her balance, pulling her face into his chest.

Cord felt her lips against his chest. Suddenly, Rosalyn looked up and reached one hand behind his neck, pulling his head down until her open mouth was on his, her tongue moving beyond his lips, slippery as a pond eel.

"I think it's time we went ashore," he said. She looked up at him and nodded.

Rosalyn popped off her bathing cap, loosening her tawny hair, and lay back on the pink blanket. Sunlight sparkled on the pond water that still beaded on her body like quicksilver gems that evaded the touch. Cord knelt beside her on the blanket as she waited expectantly. He cupped both her breasts with his hands, feeling them swell through the wet bathing suit. The tip of her tongue licked her lips as if she were savoring a special dessert.

"Wait," Rosalyn said breathlessly. She sat up and unbuttoned the top of her suit. She tried to shrug out of it, but the wet wool clung to her skin. "Help me."

Cord reached down and tugged at the suit's ruffled skirt with both hands, forcing the reluctant fabric past her waist. Rosalyn raised her slim hips and wriggled helpfully as he forced her suit past her bottom and down her thighs. Completely naked, she lay back with a shy smile, her tawny pubic hair matted and wet like a garden of golden wheat after a summer rain.

Cord shucked off his shorts and lowered himself next to her, his stiff penis prodding against her smooth thigh. Her body felt damp and slightly chilled. Tiny goosebumps stood out on her arms and stomach. She smelled watery-fresh, like a newly caught trout.

Her hand stroked his cheek as he kissed her, his tongue flicking gently across her lips. She parted her lips slightly as if she were leaving a door slightly ajar, letting his tongue deep inside her mouth and holding it captive as she clamped her teeth around it.

Cord broke off their kiss and traced his tongue down her neck until it found her swelling breast. His tongue drew a wet circle around her stiff nipple until she reached down and guided it into his mouth.

His hand strayed past her stomach as she parted her thighs to give him access to her vagina. His fingers moved into the wheat field, looking for the plowed furrow beneath.

Her eyes widened as his finger pushed past her vagina lips, plunging into her wetness up to his palm. She reached down, groping blindly for his penis, and grasped it with a hard, firm grip that almost made him cry out.

Her breath came shallow and fast as Cord worked one and then two fingers inside of her, her buttocks rising slightly to meet his hand. She moved her fist up and down his penis in the same cadence as his fingers, as if their bodies were in sweet harmony. He felt his semen rising to the surface as her vagina started to tremor.

"No," Rosalyn said in a loud voice that almost startled him. "I want you inside of me when it happens."

Cord mounted her swiftly as she parted her legs wide to make room for his body. She flung both her arms around his neck and locked her legs around his buttocks, imprisoning him in sweet feminine flesh. His penis plunged into her vagina as it came to a rolling boil. He thrust deeper, releasing his semen into her as his ball sac bumped up against her buttocks. She shuddered with pleasure, bucking her hips up to meet his thrusts as her vagina rippled along his shaft.

"That was the first time," Rosalyn sighed as they stretched out on the blanket.

The warm sun felt good against his bare skin. He felt drowsy and lazy, but he turned to her with a smile. "Normally I'd take a lady's word for a statement like that, but you seemed, well, *unsurprised* by anything that happened."

She smiled back at him. "I don't mean you took my virginity. This is the first time I've ever made love out of doors. So far, it's the best thing that's happened to me in the American West."

"That's what everyone likes about it," Cord said. "All those unexplored frontiers."

Rosalyn propped her head up on her elbow. "I have an idea. After I settle my father's estate, why don't you come east with me?"

"What about Alfred?" he asked. "He may be sophisticated, but I doubt that he'd approve of you bringing back an American lover."

She laughed out loud, a hearty laugh that he liked. "No, he wouldn't. I don't mean all the way to Europe. Come with me to New York. The train trip will take at least two weeks and we'll have another week or two before my boat sails. It would be fun, Cord Diamondback."

He shook his head. He knew he could never return to the East Coast. "What makes you think you'll have an estate to settle?"

She looked startled. "Surely you'll be ruling in my favor. I mean after what just happened."

"Is that what you expected? Were you buying my vote with your body?"

Rosalyn cast her eyes down. "No, of course not. Well, a little maybe. But I wanted sex with you too." She rose quickly and began to dress. "It's all mixed up. At the moment I wanted you, but I want what's rightfully mine too."

"I hope you won't be disappointed," Cord said. "Tomorrow, the cards will decide. In a way my judgment has already been made."

15.

Felipe came rushing around to the customer's side
of the bar almost the second Cord pushed through
the doors of the General Lew Wallace Saloon.
"Your hand, Señor Diamondback, it is all right?
There is no permanent damage?"

Cord smiled at his concern. Obviously Corazón
had held a frank chat with her hot-blooded brother.
"I'll survive, but I don't expect to win any quick-
draw contests."

"If you ever have the need of the protection of
the Lopez family . . ."

Cord stopped him. "You're overdoing the hat-in-
the-hand manner, my friend. If your apology is
sincere, I accept it."

Felipe grinned and retreated behind the bar.
"You're very clever for a gringo. If you don't care
for humble Mexicans, can I give you a drink,
courtesy of Mr. Sam Buck?"

"I'll take a beer, unless you're trying to buy my
vote."

"You are an honorable man," Felipe said, taking
him seriously. "Your decisions can't be purchased

131

for money or the kisses of a woman." He drew himself a beer and stood opposite Cord on the barman's side of the bar.

The men drank silently, Cord glad for the icy-cold liquid rolling down his throat. He realized that it had been difficult for Felipe to apologize. Pride was a part of him, as essential as his heart or liver. "Devlin says you hate Sheriff Richmond," Cord said softly. "Why is that?"

"He's a gringo." Felipe spat out the words as if they explained everything.

"That can't be the only reason."

Felipe peered into Cord's face and obviously decided to trust him. "He preys on the Mexicans in Los Gordos. Steals our money."

"Including the Lopez family?"

Felipe laughed dryly. "Particularly the Lopez family because we are the richest. Did you know that my sister pays him five hundred dollars a month?"

Cord wondered why Corazón hadn't told him that Richmond was extorting money from her. "No, I didn't. What does she get in return?"

"Richmond stays in the Anglo part of town. Before she paid him this blood money, he would come over and terrorize my people."

Cord digested the information Felipe had given him and decided it didn't quite make sense. "Corazón pays Richmond five hundred dollars a month so he won't shoot up your part of town? What about you, Felipe? I think a man with your temper and pride would try to stop him."

Felipe hung his head like a dog who'd come out second best in a backyard fight. "I tried," he whispered. "One day when the sheriff came over, I ordered him to go back. He laughed and told me to make him. Before I could draw, his gun was in his hand."

Cord nodded. He had seen Richmond's incredibly fast draw. "What happened next? Obviously he didn't shoot you."

Felipe's voice became almost inaudible. "He forced me to kneel in the dust of the street while he put the barrel of his pistol against my head. He told me to beg for mercy." Felipe glanced up, a faint spark of pride in his eyes. "I said nothing. My sister Corazón pleaded for me. When Richmond spared my life, Corazón decided to pay him the money not to return."

Felipe turned his back to hide his emotions and draw two more beers. He was still at the tap, his back toward Cord when there was a racket on the stairs. Cord glanced up to see Deuce Devlin and Maribeth Adams walking down together, heads together, smiling and self-satisfied like two swindlers who'd just unloaded a trunkful of counterfeit stock certificates. Maribeth broke off when she saw Cord and raced down the last few steps.

"Where have you been?" she asked breathlessly. "I was concerned when you didn't come back to the room last night."

Cord ignored her question and raised his beer glass toward Devlin, who bowed in return. Maribeth caught their pantomine and spun back to Cord. "What you're thinking is naughty. Deuce is merely an old friend. We were playing cribbage in my room."

"I'll bet you took him down a peg or two," Cord said. Devlin suppressed a smile.

Maribeth shook her head, puzzled. "No, Devlin won like he always does."

"What are you doing here, Devlin?" Cord suddenly asked the gambler.

"I hope that question means you're jealous," Maribeth said. She clowned an exaggerated guilty look.

"Why do you ask, Diamondback?" Devlin said cautiously. "You know I go anywhere I please."

"Yes, but what pleases you to be in Los Gordos? You're out of the poker hand because you dropped out early. What's keeping you in town?"

Devlin hesitated for a moment, chewing on the question, then a broad smile lit his face. "Curiosity," he said, his Irish brogue thickening. "Faith, and can I leave without knowing the name of the man I helped make rich?"

"Funny," Cord reflected, "you weren't curious enough on the night of the game to stay in the room for a few extra minutes and now you're waiting around for days."

Devlin eyed Cord resentfully, dropping the Irish charm. "I got you this assignment, remember? I don't like being questioned as if I'm suspected of something. Maybe I'm staying because I hope to corner the winner in another big game. Maybe I like Maribeth's company. Hell, maybe I like yours. Maybe anything. I don't answer to you, Cord Diamondback."

"You'll answer one question, Devlin, or you'll be a suspect. Give me one logical reason why you walked out of the saloon that night before the winner was decided."

Blood rose to Devlin's face. His right hand strayed toward the two-shot derringer he carried in a holster under his left armpit. Cord had seen him draw it once, fast and silent, like a striking reptile. Devlin's hand stopped near the derringer for an instant, then moved on up to his breast pocket and retrieved a packet of cheroots. He took one out and lit it carefully, using up time as if conducting a ceremony that couldn't be hurried. Finally he inhaled deeply, then made a face as if he'd swallowed rotten meat. "Stale," he said, crushing out the lighted tip on the bar. "Maribeth, honey, there's a fresh pack in the waistcoat I left hanging in your room. Be a pet and get it for me."

Maribeth hesitated, looking into the faces of Cord and Devlin, then ran upstairs. Devlin waited, posing with the bent cheroot until he heard the door shut. "I can't stand on the sidelines and watch a fixed game," he said. "It offends me."

"You have a reputation for being a smart gambler, maybe even an honest one," Cord said. "If you saw the game was fixed, why didn't you get out?"

"Because I was winning and I didn't see anything funny going on until that last hand."

Cord shook his head, still puzzled. "But you called several bets in that last hand. Why didn't you drop earlier?"

Devlin nodded, agreeing that Cord had asked an important question. "Maybe I'm losing my touch, because I never saw any evidence of tricky dealing. Of course the cards had been dealt straight all night up to the last hand, so I wasn't watching as close as I should have. When I drew four of a kind, I thought I'd make a killing. I only became suspicious when the betting got wild. What tipped me off for certain were the hand signals I spotted between two of the players."

"So I was right, my sister was cheated!" Felipe exclaimed.

Damn! Cord thought. He had forgotten that Felipe always managed to hover within earshot. No telling what the hot-blooded Mexican would do with the information. Well, it was too late to worry about him now. "If you knew the game was crooked, why didn't you register a protest? Don't tell me you were afraid of anyone sitting at that table."

Devlin frowned. "And admit I'd been slickered? I put big money into that pot before I dropped. If the word got out, I'd be laughed out of every casino in the West. I was still up a few dollars, so I figured to just walk away."

"Which players were doing the signaling?" Cord demanded.

"Hey, Devlin, I found your smokes," Maribeth Adams called triumpantly from the head of the stairs.

16.

"Pat Garrett sidles up to me one evening and whispers, 'Henry McCarty's busted out of jail again.' That was his real name you know. The Kid picked up the moniker Bill Bonney much later."

Kane Richmond had both feet propped on the unlit potbelly stove in his office, cleaning his Colt .45 and reminiscing to Cord about the old days. "When he gave me the news, Garrett shook like a man with the St. Vitus. He'd got wind that McCarty, I mean the Kid, was holed up at Maxwell's place in Fort Sumner. Pat begged me to come with him. 'The Kid's a tricky devil, but you're faster than he is.'" As he told the story, Richmond thrust the cleaning rod through the barrel of the Colt as if he were savaging a woman.

"We got to Maxwell's place about an hour before sunup. The Kid's Arabian was tied out back; he always rode the best stock, so we knew he was inside. 'You scoot on back and I'll take the front,' Garrett says to me. It was easy to see that he figured if the Kid skedaddled, he'd come running out the back, my way."

"I always heard that Garrett had two deputies with him that day," Cord interjected to prove he was paying attention.

"Frank Jessup?" Richmond recollected. "We had him staked outside watching the Kid's horse. It was the only job he'd agree to handle. Frank was too cautious a man to slip into a dark house with a killer inside."

"But not Kane Richmond?" Cord asked, deliberately feeding the sheriff lines.

Richmond shrugged proudly. "Garrett dismounted about fifty yards from the house and crawled on his belly toward the front door. I swear there was no part of the man's body that was more than three inches off the ground. I strolled around to the back on my hind legs, the way man is meant to walk, shoved my foot through a door panel, and sashayed in."

"Busting through a door when Billy Bonney might be on the other side doesn't seem a smart thing to do," Cord said.

Richmond shook his head in wonder at his daring. "If the Kid had been on the other side of that door with a twelve-gauge, I'd've eaten buckshot for breakfast."

"So how did Garrett happen to be the man who took Bonney down?"

"I told you his name was McCarty," Richmond said irritably. "Anyway, my ruckus must have scared the little bugger because I heard some scuffling, some running, and then a few shots. By the time I made my way through the house to the bedroom, young Henry McCarty, alias Billy the Kid, was lying dead with two holes in him and the great Pat Garrett was blowing smoke from the barrel of his sidearm." Richmond peered through the Colt's barrel to inspect his cleaning job. "If Garrett had made the ruckus and I'd stood my ground, I'd be a legend of the West today."

"Seems as if the incident still rankles you, Sheriff," Cord said.

Richmond appeared satisfied with his work and replaced the bullets in the chambers. During the time he had worked on the Colt another loaded gun lay within easy reach on the table. "Why shouldn't it bother me? Garrett's famous and I'm still working cowtowns, operating without any real authority. But not much longer, hey?" He looked up at Cord. "I hear you're getting them together this afternoon. That's why I'm cleaning my guns. I'll be there to back you up, partner." His cadaverous face cracked into a skull-like grin. "I can't wait until you hit Buck and Langely with the bad news."

Cord sighed. Despite his long career in law enforcement, Richmond seemed to possess only a dim idea of how the law worked. If prominent citizens like Sam Buck and Longhorn Jake Langely had their property confiscated in a dubious decision by a free-lance judge and were later found dead, there'd be an investigation. As the man who made the decision, Cord would get his share of the scrutiny. But there was no point in telling Richmond his plan wouldn't work. The man thought his idea was brilliant. That's why Cord agreed to go along with it. He needed time to think his way out of the box Richmond had put him in. One thing to his advantage: Richmond was a stupid man who thought he was clever and devious. Like most stupid men, he couldn't imagine anyone could be more devious than he.

"I figure that it'll take about thirty days to find buyers," Richmond continued. "Maybe sooner with the bargains I'll be offering. Then we'll split the money and I'm off to Mexico." He looked up at Cord. "Where you headed, partner?"

Cord shrugged. He suspected that Richmond didn't plan for him to go anywhere. Maybe the sheriff even thought about turning in Cord's corpse and claiming the reward on Christopher Deacon. "I'm glad you're going to be at the General Lew Wallace, Sheriff. No telling what Buck and Langely may do after I confiscate the pot."

"Don't you worry about them," Richmond said, patting his newly cleaned Colt. "They ain't going to bother you, or anybody else."

"But what about after the meeting this afternoon? They could come down on me hard when you're not around."

Richmond snickered. "I thought you were a tougher man, Diamondback. But you can sleep nights. Unless you're afraid of dead men coming to haunt you."

Cord walked to the door of the office and opened it. He stood with his back to the sheriff, looking out across the street toward the saloon. Richmond watched him suspiciously, but Cord kept both his hands clearly in sight, away from his Smith & Wesson.

"They all gathered at the saloon?" Richmond asked.

"Not everyone," Cord replied. He quickly stepped aside. Sam Buck, his face beaded with sweat, stood framed in the doorway, holding a double-barrel shotgun.

Richmond dropped his feet from the potbelly stove. "What the hell is this?"

"I know you're fast, Richmond, but don't try anything," Cord advised. "Sam's so nervous his finger's dancing on the trigger."

"And I'm covering you from the window," Longhorn Langely piped in.

Richmond's neck pivoted toward Langely. "What do you boys have against me?"

"Only a plot to steal our property and murder us." Sam Buck's high voice headed for the stratosphere. "In my book, that's enough reason to hold a grudge."

"You told them our plan?" Richmond asked Cord, his mouth agape. "That's stupid. You just cost yourself a hundred and fifty thousand bucks."

"I told them *your* plan," Cord said. "I don't think they liked it."

"Why the hell are we talking?" Langely groused. "Let's just shoot the son-of-a-bitch and be done with it."

"You're taking Diamondback's word against mine," Richmond protested to Sam Buck.

Sam Buck smiled tightly. "I'd take almost anyone's word against yours."

"That's enough palaver," Langely complained. "I'm coming around front to let some of the air out of this windbag."

"Wait until I've disarmed Richmond!" Cord protested. "I said two guns on him at all times." But the cowman had disappeared from the window.

Richmond tensed in his chair, his eyes half

lidded, like a snake just before it strikes. Cord pulled at his Smith & Wesson; with Langely walking around to the front door, there was only a shotgun in Sam Buck's trembling hands covering the quick-draw artist.

Richmond ignored Sam, his eyes studying Cord as his right hand rested quietly on his knee a comfortable distance from his holster. Suddenly the Colt that had been resting on the table close to the sheriff vaulted into his left hand as if it had a mind of its own.

Cord's draw had already begun, but his hand seemed to inch downward in slow motion. His gun barrel had barely cleared leather when he saw the sheriff's Colt belch fire. He snapped his head around to see Sam Buck's nose disintegrate into a shapeless, glutinous mass of flesh and blood as a .45 slug slammed into his face. The bullet sped upward, cutting a tunnel through Sam's brain, and blasted a hole out the top of his skull. Blood spurted from his bald head like a small geyser going off right on schedule. The blood seeped downward, streaking Sam's fringe of white hair red and making it look like some obscene candy cane. Sam's lifeless hands clutched the shotgun, his eyes still open in shocked and final surprise. His body crumpled to its knees and stayed there as if he were making a last prayer.

Cord saw the barrel of Richmond's Colt swing in his direction. Longhorn Langely's dismayed face appeared in the doorway for an instant then ducked back. Richmond swung the Colt toward the door, snapping off a shot at the cowman as Cord dived for the cover of a desk in the far corner of the room. A bullet sizzled past the spot he'd just vacated. Even in his predicament, Cord marveled at Richmond's ability to manipulate his weapon. A true artist. Cord realized he'd never be able to outgun the sheriff. He hunkered behind the desk, barely out of sight, as three slugs thudded into the thick oak. Thank God Richmond buys sturdy furniture, Cord thought.

Cord threw his gun hand around the desk corner and fired blind in the general direction of Richmond. Two slugs ripped into the wood near his revolver, showering his hand with wooden splinters.

Cord knew he couldn't pop his head in the open, even for an instant, without getting it blown off. There was no way he could track Richmond's movements. He raised the barrel of his Smith & Wesson over the top of the desk and fired twice more. It was like shooting into a pond and hoping to hit an unseen trout. Wishful thinking. At least his shots would keep the sheriff hopping. Two bullets skipped across the desk top like stones skipping across water and burrowed into the wall behind Diamondback.

Cord heard the report of Richmond's Colt fired in a different direction. He had obviously fired at Langely.

"You still out there, Longhorn?" Cord shouted.

"Jesus, he's killed Sam." Langely's voice quavered and almost broke.

"Get behind something and cover the door," Cord advised. "Richmond can't leave without getting past you."

"I don't know, Diamondback." Langely sounded

weak, indecisive. "If he kills you, there's no way I can handle him alone."

"Wonderful partners you picked," Richmond said scornfully. "Hey, Langely," he called out. "If you leave now, I'll let you ride away and forget this ever happened. It's Diamondback I'm after."

"Don't believe him, Longhorn," Cord called. "He can't afford to let you live. You saw him cut down Sam."

Silence from outside. Cord wondered how long the cowman would sit tight before bolting. Not long the way he spooked. Cord heard a horse neigh and a rider galloping away. The hoofbeats answered all his questions about Langely's courage.

"Seems like your buddy's gone." Richmond gloated. "That leaves you and me some time to spend together."

"Don't be too sure that Langely ran away," Cord told Richmond. "He probably went for help."

"You're scaring the hell out of me, Diamondback." Cord heard Richmond moving about the room, maneuvering for position. "Nobody in this town would dare face me down."

"What about Felipe and Devlin?" While Cord spoke, he inched toward the front edge of the desk, thinking about rolling out and risking everything on one wild shot at the sheriff.

"Naw, I took the starch out of the Mex long ago, and the Irishman won't do anything unless the odds are in his favor."

Diamondback reviewed his position and it seemed hopeless. He squatted behind a small desk in a room that his opponent knew intimately. He couldn't risk an aimed shot at Richmond without

exposing some part of his body to return fire. The
sheriff had the same problem, but at least he had
room to operate while Cord was pinned down in
two square feet of space.

Cord pulled a bullet from his gunbelt and threw it
across the room in the direction of the potbelly
stove. The bullet hit metal with a faint ring, like a
fizzled alarm, but Richmond only laughed and
jerked two shots into the desk that popped open one
of the drawers.

"I hope you got something better to offer."
Richmond snickered. "That trick was pathetic."

Cord knew he had to act fast. Sooner or later
Richmond would figure out an angle of attack that
would give him a clear shot. Maybe he would drag
out a heavier weapon that would blow the desk to
smithereens. "Hey, Richmond, how about a sport-
ing chance?"

"Huh, what do you mean?"

"You're always bragging that you're faster than
grease, well how about proving it? Holster your gun
and let me stand clear."

Richmond laughed. "I got you in a box, Diamondback. Why should I let you out?"

"No reason," Cord agreed, "except your reputation. An old-fashioned shoot-out between us would
make some news. The winner could count on some
glory."

"Not good enough. You got a reputation as a
judge, not a fast gun."

"I haven't stayed alive being slow," Cord said.
"People know that. Of course, you've already
admitted that you're not as good as you were a few

years ago. Maybe you're afraid of a man-to-man facedown."

"You can stand up anytime you feel like dying." Richmond's voice held a steel edge. "My Colts are back in their holsters."

Cord flattened his body against the floor, peering through the two-inch space at the desk's bottom. All he could see were Richmond's booted feet and his shadow caused by the morning sun streaming through the one window. That long extension of the sheriff's arm must be his Colt, still in his hand. So much for the promise of a fair fight. Cord placed his Smith & Wesson on the floor, rolling it on the side to get the barrel in the small air space under the desk.

"Where the hell are you, Diamondback? I ain't going to wait forever."

"Just getting up my nerve, Sheriff," Cord said. He squinted, aiming the barrel as best he could toward Richmond's left boot. "Here I come," Cord called. He saw the shadow arm point at desk-top level. He knew that once an inch of his head was exposed, Richmond would blow it off. He took a deep breath and squeezed the trigger of his Smith & Wesson. The gun exploded so close to his ear he didn't hear Richmond's roar of pain or the clatter of his Colt falling to the floor.

Cord scrambled to his feet and raced around the desk. Richmond sat dazed on the floor, the heel of his left boot shot away and a small trickle of blood soaking through the lawman's sock.

"Damn, you've blown my foot away!" Richmond cursed as Cord relieved the sheriff of his second Colt.

"I barely grazed your heel." Cord laughed. "You'll be limping for a week and that's all."

"What happens now?" Richmond asked. "You gonna plug me and then brag you outdrew Kane Richmond?"

"I'm locking you up in your own jail," Cord said. "I imagine the sheriff in Fort Sumner will be picking you up for Sam Buck's murder."

"Don't you think you can lock me up and walk away from me, Diamondback," Richmond said, his knuckles deadly white as his fists gripped the cell bars. "I'm like Henry McCarty; no jail can hold me. I'm walking out of here, and when I do, you're a dead man."

"Here's an extra blanket," Cord said, throwing it to Richmond between the bars. "I know from experience this place gets damn cold at night."

Cord stepped around Sam Buck's corpse, which was still kneeling in the jail doorway. He was late for the meeting in the General Lew Wallace and he didn't want to keep Tim Brady's murderer waiting.

17.

"I rushed in here to get you help," Longhorn Langely said, first looking startled and then sheepish as Cord burst through the batwing doors of the General Lew Wallace Saloon.

Felipe had a 12-gauge shotgun trained on the cowman. "He tried to remove the bill of sale for his cattle from the poker table," the Mexican explained.

"I was afraid Richmond would storm in here and take everything," Langely said. "Those cattle are mine anyway. I was getting around to asking for help."

Deuce Devlin sat at a small corner table playing blackjack with Maribeth Adams. He looked up lazily. "Longhorn didn't request any assistance. Help for what?"

"Richmond killed Sam Buck," Cord said. "I just put the sheriff in jail."

Langely's beefy face lit up to the color of a medium-ripe tomato. "You took Kane Richmond? Damn fine job, Diamondback. I think you just earned yourself a bonus."

Felipe turned over the shotgun to Cord. "I will pay our sheriff a visit so he doesn't get lonely."

"Stay here," Cord ordered. "We finish the poker game today just as soon as everyone's here."

Rosalyn Brady and Corazón Lopez walked in together holding an animated conversation. They saw Cord and quickly stopped talking. Rosalyn flushed.

"We're all here now," Langely said, suddenly full of enthusiasm. "Let's get the game over with so I can put my cattle on my new ranch."

"There's no reason for us to stay," Felipe told his sister. "You didn't cover the last bet, and Señor Diamondback has ruled the players' money will not be returned. What difference does it make to us which gringo wins the pot?"

Cord glanced at Felipe, almost amused by the Mexican's overbearing pride. "You may be interested in the outcome. Perhaps it will be different than you expected."

"The losers are always crying," Langely said gleefully. "Let's get on with the game." He unconsciously rubbed his hands in anticipation.

Cord faced the players. "Two days ago I delayed finishing the game because I needed certain information. I now have it, so everyone back to the poker table in the seats you held that night."

"If you're trying to recreate the original positions, you'll have to drag over Sam Buck's body and dig up Tim Brady," Devlin said.

Cord grinned at Devlin. "Thanks for the suggestion, Deuce. I'll draw to Brady's hand."

"I'll play my father's cards." Rosalyn Brady bristled.

"You don't know anything about poker," Cord said softly. "I have my reasons for doing it this way. You sit on the sidelines and be quiet."

"That's special treatment," Langely protested. "How can you be an impartial judge when you're holding down a seat in the game? Hell, you might switch the rules."

"Standard poker rules will apply, nothing else."

"What about Sam's hand?" Langely asked. "He's got a draw coming."

"Before I decide that, let's review the betting on that last round." Cord looked toward Langely. "That's a standard poker rule. I believe that Sam Buck started that last round of bets when he raised Langely's wager of five hundred dollars by putting up the stock in his freight line."

"That's right," Devlin said. "Up to then it was just another card game."

"Corazón, you were next and dropped?"

"Yes," she said. "I had a good hand, but I wasn't willing to gamble my life's work in a card game."

"Devlin, you threw in your cards?"

Devlin nodded. "Stakes were too high for me."

"Then Brady called Sam Buck by putting up his ranch and Langely anted his herd of cattle. Right so far? Was that the situation when Brady was shot?"

"We told you all that before," Langely said, impatiently drumming his fingers against the green felt table. "Please, let's complete the draw and decide the winner once and for all."

"Not yet," Cord said. "I'm afraid the betting on that last round was improper."

"Improper!" Langely roared. "How? Everyone at the table agreed to the stakes."

"When Brady put up his ranch and Langely threw in his herd, they thought they were matching the value of Sam's freight line. But I just got a reply to a wire I sent two days ago. Sam's line is worthless. I became suspicious when Sam tried to sell it to Corazón Lopez. The railroad is laying tracks between Los Gordos and Santa Fe. Mule-driven wagons can't compete for freight with railroad cars. Sam was unloading his teams for the past two months. They're all sold now except for one team he keeps in Los Gordos for show. That one mule team and wagon is the entire value of his company."

"Then Sam didn't make the big bet everyone thought he did?" Devlin asked.

"You see the implication?" Cord said. "He bet his freight line. That's one wagon and six mules. I figure they're worth about a thousand dollars."

"This is preposterous," Langely sputtered. "Sam showed me and Tim independent appraisals."

"All made before the railroad announced their plans to move this way."

"A bet's a bet," Langely insisted.

Devlin shook his head, helping out Cord. "Not when it's made with worthless stock. Same thing as betting with counterfeit money."

Cord nodded. "I'm giving everyone, including the players who dropped, a chance to revise their final bet based on the true value of Sam's freight line."

All the players except Deuce Devlin dived

toward their cards. They labored strenuously to extract the ten-penny nails that had been driven through the pasteboards into the wooden table. Langely, cursing, slipped a coin under the nail head, slowly prying it loose. Corazón used her fingers and joined Langely in cursing when one of her long fingernails broke off. Cord smiled and reached under the table with his Smith & Wesson, using the butt to pound the nail up out of the wood. He left Brady's hand on the table without glancing at it.

"Any tampering with the cards?" he asked as the players stared at their hands. There was no answer. "Good. Let's proceed."

Devlin stood holding the back of his chair, a half-smoked cheroot on his lips. "Not interested, Devlin?" Cord asked.

The Irishman shrugged. "I threw my cards in the middle when I dropped. Besides, some people at this table have shown an awesome confidence in their holdings."

"In that case, would you mind taking Sam Buck's hand? Play it as well as you can."

"This is absurd!" Langely roared.

"Why?" Cord asked. "Sam's estate has the finest cardplayer in the West protecting its interests."

"Thanks for the compliment," Devlin said, easing into Sam's seat. He repeated Cord's trick of using the butt of his revolver to hammer up the ten-penny nail that fastened his cards. When he picked up Sam's hand, his face broke into a huge grin.

Cord finally slid Tim Brady's hand toward his chest, holding the cards close as he inspected them.

Four aces twinkled at him. The hand was just what he had expected. "You have another chance to call," he reminded Corazón Lopez. "The bet is one thousand dollars."

Corazón picked up her cards and examined them with new interest. She eyed the other players, looked toward Felipe, and finally reached for her purse. "I'll risk another wager."

"Don't listen to the gringo," Felipe said, his dark face turning brownish purple. "This is just another ruse to steal more Lopez money."

Cord glanced over at Corazón a little surprised. While he had to give her the opportunity, he hadn't expected her to call the bet. He looked at his four aces again, threw some blue chips into the pot, and pulled out one of the legal documents. "The Brady estate withdraws the deed to the ranch and calls Sam's thousand-dollar bet."

Longhorn Jake Langely sat slumped in his chair, peering at his cards. He looked sullen and morose but suddenly brightened as he thought of something. "It's my turn," he cried, "and I raise my seven thousand head of cattle." His eyes glittered triumphantly as he obviously believed he'd spotted a loophole. "Under the rules, you can't stop me from raising any amount I like."

Cord nodded. "You can push the stakes right back up to where they were. And I guarantee that I'll call you, just the way Tim Brady would have. But before you bet everything you own, you should know that I plan on taking advantage of another poker rule."

"What's that?" Langely asked scornfully. "You

can't tell me the value of my cattle doesn't match Brady's ranch."

"I'm sure it does, Langely," Cord said. "But I'm not talking about the value of your wager, I'm referring to poker procedure. A player can call for a cut of the deck at any time. I'm going to exercise that privilege before the cards are dealt."

Langely's mouth dropped open, showing teeth badly in need of dental work. His overweight body slumped as if he'd been hit by a rifle slug.

Maribeth Adams broke the silence. "Are you accusing me of something, Cord Diamondback? I mean requesting a cut of the cards in the middle of the game reflects on the dealer's honesty. Remember, Deuce Devlin was sitting in that game and he didn't see anything illegal. Did you, Deuce honey?"

Devlin shrugged his shoulders eloquently.

"Did you still want to raise, Langely?" Cord asked, ignoring Maribeth.

"I call the thousand-dollar bet," the cattleman said. He reached in the pot and withdrew his bill of sale for his herd of cattle.

"Pot's all right?" Cord asked. He motioned to Maribeth, who angrily slapped down the deck in front of him. Cord carefully cut the cards in the middle and watched Maribeth as she replaced the two parts. "Deal."

"Cards please." Maribeth hissed the words.

Corazón Lopez chewed on her lower lip as she considered her hand. "I'll take one card," she said finally.

Both Cord and Deuce Devlin followed Maribeth Adams's hands as she dealt the cards. The room was cool, but Cord could see a thin trickle of sweat break through her face powder like a small crack in an earthen dam.

"How many cards, Deuce?" she asked. Her voice almost broke.

Deuce scratched his head, "I'll take two," he said casually.

"Sam bet a freight company on three of a kind?" Cord asked. "He must have been a plunger." Cord's suspicions on how the hand had been rigged to swindle Tim Brady were now confirmed.

Cord reviewed his own cards and examined his four sweet aces. It was the sort of hand to entice a man into betting a ranch. Almost a no-lose proposition. *Almost.* "I'll have one card," Cord said, throwing away a useless tray and drawing an equally useless ten spot.

Langely's face reddened like a hazy sunset. "I'll take one card." He snatched the card from the table and quickly buried it in his hand. Langely looked up impatiently. "No more pussyfooting. Let's turn up the cards."

"You don't seem as confident as you did a few minutes ago," Cord observed. "But you're forgetting something. There's another round of betting after the draw."

"Oh, for God's sake let's forget about the rules and get this game over with," Langely cried.

"The rules were important to you earlier," Cord reminded him. "Deuce, you're betting Sam's hand and he was the opener. What do you do?"

Devlin studied his cards through lidded eyes. "Pass," he finally said. He threw his cards in the middle. "This hand isn't worth anything."

Corazón Lopez still chewed her lips. "I believe I'm next?" She opened her purse, avoiding Felipe's eyes. "I bet fifty dollars."

"You're crazy!" Felipe shouted at her.

"You've surprised me a second time," Cord told her. First she had stayed in the game when he hadn't expected it and now she placed a small bet as if deliberately provoking a big raise. Cord threw one of Brady's remaining chips into the pot. "I call your fifty."

Longhorn Langely cradled his cards in his huge hands, slowly pinching them open one by one. He heaved a sigh and squeezed the last card for what seemed an eternity.

"The bet is fifty dollars; it's up to you, Langely," Cord said.

Langely finally uncovered his last card and his face fell like a small landslide. "Busted," he said, throwing his cards across the room. "Busted."

"Worth seven thousand head of cattle before the draw and not fifty dollars afterward? You're not much of a poker player, Langely."

"Shut your trap," Langely said angrily.

Cord smiled across the table toward Corazón. "We're the only ones left and I won't keep you in suspense." He threw up his cards. "Four aces."

"I told you we would be cheated again," Felipe said.

Corazón frowned. She slowly laid down her cards one at a time until five diamonds, from the four through the eight, rested on the table. "Not good enough," she said proudly. "I have a straight flush."

18.

"We won?" Felipe asked, not believing the evidence. "We won?"

Stunned, Cord examined Corazón's cards and then laughed out loud. He had outsmarted a swindle only to be beaten by a player who was supposed to play a minor role. He realized he could never be a professional gambler like Devlin. There were too many imponderables for his orderly mind. He shook his head sadly. "First time I've ever held four aces and I've been beaten."

"Cord, will you please tell me what happened?" Rosalyn Brady asked.

Cord laughed again. "You still have the ranch, but you won't be bringing Alfred the size dowry you hoped for."

"Game's over, so I'll be getting along," Langely said, rising rapidly from his chair.

"You can wait right here," Cord told Langely. "Corazón might be interested in how she won this pot."

"I won it with a small straight flush," Corazón

said, looking up as Felipe helped her gather money and chips into a saddlebag.

"You were the beneficiary of a swindle," Cord told the Mexican woman. "When Sam Buck's finances went sour, he developed a scheme to cheat Tim Brady out of his ranch. He enlisted Longhorn Jake Langely who went along because his cattle needed Brady's water."

"What I gonna do about them critters now?" Langely mumbled.

"Sam hired the slickest dealer in the West, Maribeth Adams, to deal the game. Deuce Devlin was invited to give the game respectability. If he didn't see anything out of hand, then everyone would assume the game was honest."

"Being an authority is a heavy burden," Devlin said.

"He didn't see any evidence of misdealing," Maribeth said hotly. "No seconds, no dealing off the bottom."

"She's right," Devlin offered.

"That's because Maribeth dealt only from the top," Cord said. "Devlin, do you remember leaving the table just before the final hand?"

"Sure," Devlin said. "I threw in my cards the previous round and went to the bar for a beer."

"That's when Maribeth switched to a stacked deck. She's so quick only you could have seen her do it."

"A stacked deck!" Devlin shook his head in disbelief. "Maribeth, I'm disappointed in you."

Maribeth pouted prettily but kept her mouth shut.

Cord continued. "Every card in that deck was placed in position for a specific purpose: to lure

Brady into betting his ranch. Even the seating was arranged to squeeze Brady. Sam sat in front of him and Langely behind. Brady was dealt four aces and Sam threw out the bait by betting his freight line. Brady snapped at it by offering his ranch. What he didn't know was that Langely had been dealt a four-card straight flush.''

"That's what I was dealt," Corazón exclaimed.

"Yes, but a smaller one than Langely's," Cord told her. "I told you every hand was rigged. They wanted every player in the game as long as possible to build up the pot."

"If the deck was stacked, why not give Langely all five cards for his flush?" Corazón asked.

"To rope the sucker in," Devlin interrupted. "They wanted to milk him for as much as they could get. Brady held four aces. When he saw everyone else drawing cards, he knew he held the winner going into the draw. Maybe they could lure him into betting still more."

"Yup," Cord agreed. "Maribeth, you did a beautiful job. I hope you were well paid."

"One thousand dollars," Maribeth said proudly. "And they got their money's worth. Devlin didn't suspect a thing until the betting got wild."

"I think I see," Corazón said. "When you cut the cards, you disturbed positions. You kept Langely from getting the fifth card to complete his straight flush."

Cord nodded. "And I cut right into *your* straight flush."

Corazón looked over at Langely sadly. "Longhorn, I never thought you could murder anyone."

"Who said anything about murder?" Langely looked shocked.

"Buck and Langely didn't conspire in Brady's death," Cord said. "His shooting messed up their plans. They would have succeeded with their swindle if Brady had stayed alive."

"Thank heavens you're not trying to saddle us with that," Langely said bitterly. "Kane Richmond must have been the killer. He's the only one in town who's a good-enough marksman."

"I don't think so," Cord said. "Richmond told me he entered the saloon a few minutes before the shooting. I believe him."

"Yeah, you're right," Devlin said. "I passed him coming in on my way out for some fresh air. That was before the shooting. Besides, what motive did Richmond have to kill Brady?"

"What motive did anyone have?" Cord asked. "It was in everyone's interests to keep Brady alive."

"Not Rosalyn Brady," Langely said thoughtfully. "She wanted that dowry."

"How dare you accuse me of killing my father," Rosalyn shouted. "I loved him."

"No," Cord said softly. "Rosalyn was back at her ranch when it happened. Felipe rode out after the shooting and found her there. He's a much faster rider than an inexperienced young woman who was raised on the Continent."

"Then who the hell shot him?" Langely asked. "And why?"

"Someone who was aiming at another person," Cord said. "Felipe, you went outside to discuss something with your sister?"

"That's right," Corazón confirmed. "We talked about the value of Sam's freight line."

"But before Felipe returned to the saloon, he saw Richmond walk in the door. He hated Richmond."

"He's a gringo killer who robbed my people, but I didn't shoot at him," Felipe said. He came out from behind the bar and faced Cord, his hands knotted into fists.

"You wanted him dead because he was taking money from your sister. The bribes weren't to protect the Mexican part of town, they were to keep you alive."

"Yes," Corazón whispered. "Richmond threatened to kill Felipe unless I paid him."

"Felipe's pride couldn't take that," Cord said. "When he saw Richmond standing next to the poker table, he pressed up against the saloon window and took a shot at him. But the night was dark and the rainfall heavy. The distance from window to table was about forty feet. Felipe shot at Richmond but hit Brady."

The Mexican was silent. "I'm sorry for that," he finally said. "Brady had done me no wrong."

Corazón let out a small sob. "Felipe, you did this?"

"That's why Felipe rode out to Brady's ranch to tell Rosalyn her father was dead. He felt remorse over the accident."

"I meant to kill Richmond," Felipe said in a husky whisper.

"That makes it murder," Cord said. "Accident or not."

"Yes," Felipe said, "but I won't let you arrest

me. I know a Mexican can't get justice in a gringo court."

Cord put both his hands on the poker table where Felipe could see them. "It's not my job to bring you in."

"You're letting him go?" Rosalyn demanded. "He killed my father."

"Do you want to see him hanged for an accident?" Cord asked her. "He's right about the kind of justice he'll get in an American border town."

"I don't know," she wailed. Her face turned red. "I hate this primitive place!"

Cord looked Felipe square in the eye. "There's no warrant for you, *yet*."

Felipe nodded. "By the time there is, I will be in Sonora." He hugged Corazón.

Corazón held her brother's face in her hands. "When will I see you again?"

Felipe shrugged. "Come to Sonora." He trotted to the door and looked back at Rosalyn. "I am truly sorry, señorita." He glanced up at Cord. "Adios, gringo."

"You're some judge," Langely said. "Letting murderers go free. What are your plans for me? Not that you can prove any of this unless Maribeth is dumb enough to testify."

"I don't have to prove anything," Cord said. "I was paid to pick the winner of a poker game, nothing more. When the story gets around, I don't imagine your reputation will improve."

Langely rose from the table. "You ain't seen the last of me, Diamondback. I'm remembering this."

Corazón Lopez put her hand on Cord's arm. "You helped me win the poker game, but you also cost me the company of my brother. I don't know whether to thank or curse you."

"Come back with me to the ranch," Rosalyn asked him. "Help me set a fair price."

"I'll be there later," Cord said. "First I'm riding to Fort Sumner to tell the authorities about Kane Richmond."

Langely stopped near the saloon's entrance and peered outside. "No need to wear out any saddle leather." There was a gloat in the cattleman's voice.

"Cord Diamondback!" a voice roared from the street. "It's me, Kane Richmond. Did you think I wouldn't know how to break out of my own jail? Now come out here and face me man to man."

19.

Cord carefully peered through the batwing doors of the General Lew Wallace. Kane Richmond stood facing the saloon, his legs anchored a foot apart, small eddies of dust swirling around his boots. Twin Colt .45s rode low on his hips; his hands appeared frozen in space a few inches from the glistening handles.

"Time to face up, Diamondback," Richmond called to the saloon. "Who knows? Maybe you got a chance. I told you I'm not as fast as I was five years ago."

Cord remembered Richmond drawing down on him a few days ago, his quicksilver hands faster than the eye could follow. "I could use some help with him," he told Langely.

Langely snorted. "You expect help from me? I hope Richmond shoots you to pieces."

"When he finishes with me, he may come after you," Cord said. "You helped me put him in jail."

"Nothing's getting me out there." Langely shook his head determinedly. "Richmond's the best man with a gun I ever saw. He'd probably take both of us down."

"Someone must stay here and record your triumph," Devlin said before Cord had a chance to ask him for help.

"Don't go out there," Corazón pleaded.

"There's no point in waiting for him to come in here." Cord carefully checked his Smith & Wesson.

"You can't stand up against him straight on," Corazón said. "No one can."

Cord picked up a carbine from behind the bar. "Who said anything about straight on?" he asked as he slid out the side door.

Watch for
RIVER RACE VERDICT

fifth novel in the Diamondback series

coming in September!

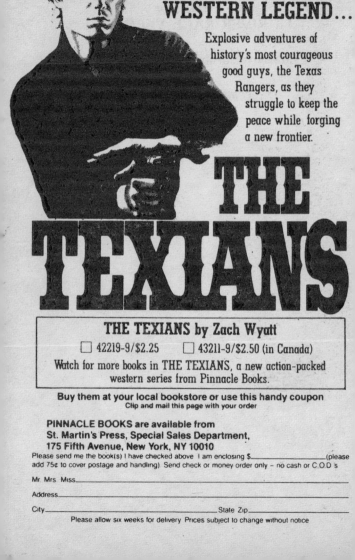